D0065651

This Is Not the Abby Show

Debbie Reed Fischer

THiS iS NOT THE ABBY SHOW

Delacorte Press

Text copyright © 2016 by Debbie Reed Fischer
Jacket art copyright © 2016 by Tuesday Mourning

Published in the United States by Delacorte Press,
an imprint of Random House Children's Books,
a division of Penguin Random House LLC, New York.
Delacorte Press is a registered trademark and the colophon
is a trademark of Penguin Random House LLC.

Visit us on the Web! randomhousekids.com

Educators and librarians, for a variety of teaching tools, visit us at
RHTeachersLibrarians.com

Library of Congress Cataloging-in-Publication Data
Names: Fischer, Debbie Reed.
Title: This is not the Abby show / Debbie Reed Fischer.
Description: First edition. | New York : Delacorte Press, [2016] | Summary:
"A girl with ADHD loves to make people laugh, but when her acting out gets
her stuck in summer school, she will have to try her hardest to turn over a
new leaf"— Provided by publisher.
Identifiers: LCCN 2016008026 | ISBN 978-0-553-53634-8 (hardback) |
ISBN 978-0-553-53636-2 (glb) | ISBN 978-0-553-53635-5 (ebook)
Subjects: | CYAC: Attention-deficit hyperactivity disorder—Fiction. | Schools—
Fiction. | Summer—Fiction. | Jews—United States—Fiction. | Humorous
stories. | BISAC: JUVENILE FICTION / Humorous Stories. | JUVENILE
FICTION / Family / Multigenerational. | JUVENILE FICTION / Social
Issues / Friendship.
Classification: LCC PZ7.F498764 Th 2016 | DDC [Fic]—dc23
LC record available at http://lccn.loc.gov/2016008026

The text of this book is set in 11-point Palatino.
Interior design by Trish Parcell

Printed in the United States of America
10 9 8 7 6 5 4 3 2 1
First Edition

For Eric, the love of my life, who supports me in every possible way. I love you.

♡

1

Pretty much everything I do is inappropriate.

How come I haven't been discovered by talent scouts yet? It is the big mystery of my life.

Maybe it's because I'm stuck in Poco Bay, Florida, surrounded by suburbanoids. I should be in Hollywood on the set of my own TV show, not sitting here like a wilting plant in Mr. Finsecker's class. He's the meanest teacher in the whole seventh grade. Right now he's practically having a seizure because I don't have my homework, even though I told him I did it.

"It's in here somewhere," I say, pulling out two old, crumpled English tests from deep inside my backpack (one C−, one D). So far I've found lip balm, hair bands, a gummy bear with a penny stuck to it, my school ID, five broken pencils, and a pair of PE shorts I've been missing since spring break.

"Abby Green, if horse manure were music, you'd be a symphony." Finsecker is always saying stuff like that. No one ever knows what he's talking about. Especially me.

Emptying my backpack in front of everyone feels like stripping off my jeans and performing a little undies dance, which is something I like to do at sleepovers. Embarrassing. But funny.

I'll do *anything* for funny.

Except I don't love people seeing what a secret slob I am. Silent Amy is watching me with caution and curiosity, the way you might look at someone with a face tattoo. I bet her pretty pink backpack is filled with heart-covered notebooks and candy-scented erasers.

Finsecker glares down at my mess. His ears have gray hair balls, as if someone stuffed dryer lint in there. If I ever grow hairy ear shrubs, I'll wax them off like my mom does to her lady mustache.

I pull out a random piece of paper all folded up and hand it to him. "Here's my homework."

Finsecker unfolds it. Crumbs rain down onto the linoleum tile, filling the air with the unmistakable scent of Fritos. I spot the half-eaten bag, take it out, and wave it around. "Anybody want a Frito?" The back row is giggling like crazy.

2

"I'll take one!" Caitlin calls out. Caitlin's my best friend. We used to sit next to each other, but Finsecker separated us for horsing around.

He ignores Caitlin, pulls the paper flat, and reads, "Yo momma's so dumb she gets lost in thought." Everyone laughs.

"Oh, yeah, that's, uh . . . for a different class," I say. "Creative writing."

"You don't take creative writing," Finsecker says. "I teach it, and I'm certain you are not in it." He crumples up the paper. "That's a zero." The giggles stop. It gets quiet. Uncomfortably quiet.

Another zero. Because he thinks *I'm* a zero.

My face burns. What does he know? I'm gifted in math and science, but Finsecker only cares about English. Now he's going off about how the inmates aren't going to run the asylum. He talks slower than an ice cube melts.

In two weeks, this torture will be over. Good-bye Palm Middle School, hello Camp Star Lake for the Performing Arts, my first step toward becoming an actress. At school I always get the roles with lines that make the audience fall out of their seats laughing, like Rizzo in *Grease* last month. I hope I get the same kind of parts at camp.

When I was little, I used to pretend I was the star of a TV show called *The Abby Show*, which I "performed" for an audience of stuffed animals. It was

3

a combo of comedy sketches and interviews with famous people. Sometimes I'd interview myself and play both parts. I still make up crazy characters and do accents at dinner, until Mom or Dad goes, "Enough! This is not the Abby show!"

It doesn't faze me. Someday there *will* be *The Abby Show.*

Finsecker is still blah-blahing. White, cotton-bally things are gathered in the corners of his mouth. If I offered to get him a drink, he'd yell at me for not paying attention. He doesn't understand that I *do* pay attention, just not to the same things as everyone else. For instance, yesterday, I noticed that Brett's eyes are the exact same blue as Windex. He made it into Star Lake too, another reason I'm dying to get there already.

Finsecker's lips are moving, but whatever he's saying is white noise. I mind surf when I get bored, which happens a lot in this class because Finsecker is a human sleeping pill, and because of my Attention Deficit/Hyperactivity Disorder. I have the type of ADHD boys usually have, the hyperactive/impulsive variety. Girls typically have the spacey, able-to-sit-in-your-seat kind. I'm spacey too, but some part of my body is always moving.

Now, for instance, I'm squirming like a caught fish. I need to get up, but if I go sharpen my pencil, Finsecker will probably stab me with it.

"NOW!" Finsecker yells.

"Aaah!" I yell back, startled. My knee bangs the underside of my desktop. "Ow!" I have no idea what he just said, but a lot of people are laughing, so I cross my eyes and force out a chuckle. Here comes a new bruise. The pain is *blinding.*

"Good one, klutz!" Caitlin calls out. "Abs the Spabz again!" Some friend. Who is she to call me a klutz? I'm the one who made the soccer team, not her.

Taptaptap. Finsecker has this annoying habit of tapping the board with his marker. If he had bothered to read my Individual Education Plan (IEP), he would know that I find repetitive noises HIGHLY distracting.

My eyes stray and land on Trina Vargas sitting next to me. She's wearing pajama pants with monkeys on them, plus she forgot her shoes again. Does Trina just roll out of bed and come to school, or what? Our school may not require uniforms, but it does require shoes. It's amazing how many classes Trina goes to before a teacher finally notices she doesn't have shoes on and sends her to the office.

One of Trina's socks has a hole in it. Her big toe is sticking out. She sees me looking, wiggles it, smiles. It's so funny. A giggle escapes out of the basement of my belly. Then another. And another. Once I get started, I can't stop.

This always happens at the worst times, like in

synagogue or at the doctor's or in the principal's office. It's really inappropriate. Pretty much everything I do is inappropriate.

My giggling goes viral.

"SETTLE DOWN!" Finsecker yells. I clap my hand over my mouth. He points at me. "You are purposely disrupting my class."

I waggle my purple pen back and forth at lightning speed. "I resent the insinuendo!"

And then it happens.

My pen flies out of my hand, whirling through the air like a helicopter wing.

Thwack.

Magic Max Finkelstein gets it right between the eyes. The back row explodes in laughter. Max's blond, wavy-haired head bobs up from his laptop screen, dazed. He rubs the red mark on his forehead where the pen hit him. "Sorry!" I call out to him. Max is new this year, and nobody knows much about him, except that he's obsessed with magic. He spends most of his time looking up magic tricks on his laptop, pretending he's taking notes.

"Well, Miz Green," says Finsecker. "Regardless of how you feel about my *insinuation,* you are one final exam away from failing. Flunking. Do you hear me?"

Flunking? Because of a few missing assignments? A prickly heat spreads across my face. Why did he have to say that in front of the whole class?

Everyone is watching me, but not like before when it felt good, when I was cracking jokes and getting laughs. I slide down in my seat and hide behind my long brown hair. There's a faint scratch carved into my desk. Right now I wish I could be like that scratch and blend into the background. If only I was a blending-into-the-background kind of girl. But I'm not. I'm a one-of-these-things-is-not-like-the-others type, the type that's born to stand out.

That's the problem.

2

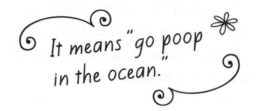

Finsecker writes on the board:

Abby said she would hand in her homework on Monday.

"Identify the misplaced modifier, Miz Green."

The only things I can identify are the insults in my head. According to my grandpa, the absolute worst insult in Yiddish is *gay kocken offen yam.* It means "go poop in the ocean." Who came up with that dis? It's not even an insult. It's more of a suggestion, really.

Taptaptap. Chairs creak as kids shift in their

seats, waiting for me to give an answer. I comfort myself with the thought that surfaces every time this happens: *When I'm famous, you'll all brag that you knew me.*

Misplaced modifier. Sounds familiar. I think that was in last night's homework. Which, as has been established, I didn't finish.

Or do at all, to be honest. Because when Finsecker was assigning it, I was watching Trina doodle dragons. Then this kid kept sniffing every two seconds, and I was going crazy wanting to tell him to go blow his nose already. Then the period was over, and I forgot to get the homework from Caitlin.

I wish Finsecker's class wasn't before lunch, when my meds don't—

Wait. Did I take my pill this morning?

Uh-oh. No, I didn't. I forgot. Again. This morning I was playing a game on my phone instead of eating breakfast, so I didn't pay attention to my pill or my Cheerios. I've kinda been doing that a lot lately.

Great.

Mom will see the yellow pill on the kitchen table. It will be "the last straw," and tomorrow she'll go back to leaving me babyish Post-its with messages like *Good morning, Abbles! This is your friendly reminder to take your medicine* ☺. Or worse, she'll sit next to me, sipping her coffee, watching me like a hawk so

I can't do what I like to do in the morning, which is play on my phone at the table, sit with my feet up, and pour sugar into my cereal instead of honey.

I am never going to hear the end of this.

The thing is, there isn't a pill or a patch in the world that completely cures ADHD. Believe me. I've tried a lot of them. Some work great for focus but don't let me eat or sleep. Others give me headaches or stomach pains. Now I'm on a good med with the only side effect being that sometimes I have no appetite, but it only works for a few hours at a time, so I take one in the morning and one after lunch.

Max is mouthing something to me. *Ah, money.* What? Oh! *On Monday.*

"On Monday!" I shout. "That's the answer. On Monday."

Surprise and irritation pass over Finsecker's face. "Correct." When he turns around to erase what he's written on the board, I mouth "thank you" to Max. He always knows the right answer but never seems to be paying attention. Sometimes I spot him with his dad at the pool in my development. We act like we don't see each other, although you can't miss him because he's so tall. It's awkward enough to be caught in public with your parents when you're twelve, let alone while wearing a bathing suit.

"Explain to us, Miz Green, how you found the misplaced modifier. Hmm?"

If I make a joke, they won't notice I'm lost. "I never misplaced the modifier, so it was easy to find."

"What?"

"I never misplaced it, know what I mean? I knew where it was the whole time." Everyone laughs, even Silent Amy.

Finsecker points to the door. "Get out of my class."

Okay, not quite everyone.

"Get out! Get out! GET! OUT!"

"You want me to get out?"

"Yes! You have earned yourself a detention. Wednesday."

This day is getting better and better.

He starts to mark it down in his book, then stops and rubs his chin. "Did you know you've already had two detentions this semester?"

Of course I know. I got the first one when we had a sub and I wrote *Primrose Everdeen* on the attendance sheet and then screamed "I VOLUNTEER AS TRIBUTE!" when she called the name. The second time was because Finsecker saw me pull the *S* off the art teacher's SCRAP ART bulletin board. Not exactly federal offenses.

Finsecker rubs his chin some more. "After two detentions, a third offense is a *suspension.*"

WHAT? He can't do that. Suspension is a *serious* punishment for *bad* kids.

I'm not a bad kid. "Please, don't," I beg. "It's almost

11

the last week of school. I'll make up the work. I promise. I'm sorry. Please."

Mr. Finsecker turns around and starts erasing the board. I can hear my heart pounding. I stuff my books and papers back into my bag, zip it, and sling it over my shoulder. *I will not cry. That's what he wants.* Head held high, I walk slowly out of the room, partly because my knee is killing me, partly to show I don't care.

But I do. Everyone will talk about me behind my back after I leave. I can already feel the glances and whispers. Silent Amy turns all the way around in her seat to watch me go. A couple of the nicer kids whisper, "Sorry, Abby," as I pass their desks. I don't open my mouth to say thanks, because my lower lip is starting to tremble.

When I get to the girls' bathroom, I lock myself in a stall, kick the toilet-seat cover down, and sit. My shoulders slump, giving way to big, heaving sobs. I cover my face, trying to hold my tears in, but they come out anyway. My fingers get all wet.

I've been lying to my parents about my English grades for months. Now I might flunk *and* get suspended.

What am I going to do?

3

*I am a genius.
Earlier in the day
I was an idiot.
That's how it is
with me.*

My mother thinks she's always right.

I know this because she says "I'm always right" approximately fifty times a day. She's saying it to me now. "I'm always right. I knew your Aunt Roz wouldn't come to your brother's bar mitzvah." She rips open another RSVP envelope right here on the sidewalk in front of our mailbox, too bar mitzvah–crazed to go inside and open them in the kitchen like a normal person.

I'm right about a lot too, like the fact that she's on a need-to-know basis about my English grades and possible suspension. So far Finsecker hasn't called, but I'm worried he might, so I have a plan to get my parents to a loud restaurant tonight where they'll never hear their phones. Then maybe Finsecker will come to his senses and forget the whole thing.

Mom slides another RSVP card back in its envelope. "I bet you Roz is still swollen from her facelift. That's why she's not coming to see her nephew become a man."

I dribble my basketball on the driveway. My knee is turning blue-black where I hit it against my desk in class, but it's not swollen. "I don't understand how reading the Bible in Hebrew turns Drew into a man."

Mom shrugs. "Ask the rabbi."

"Drew is only thirteen. How is that a man? He still collects Star Wars figures. He drinks Juicy Juice."

"So do you, so I wouldn't talk," I hear Drew say as the garage door opens. He comes out, aiming his precious video camera at me. Drew films everything. He even filmed Mom waving my pill at me when I got home from school. (We're going back to Post-its. I didn't fight it.)

I dribble, spin, and shoot. *Swoosh!* It goes in perfectly. I glance at Mom to see if she saw it. She didn't.

Mom adjusts the strap of her new sparkly tank top. Yesterday, when I saw it in the shopping bag on her bed, I thought it was for me. Wrong. "Abby, want to come to the mall with me this weekend? You need a dress for the bar mitzvah."

"I already picked a dress, remember?" I dribble backward.

Mom jumps out of the way. "Twelve-year-olds do not wear backless dresses. It's inappropriate."

"Mom, did you *watch* the Teen Choice Awards? They do too!"

"Don't raise your voice to me, please."

"Sorry. Bad day." Epic understatement of the year. As far as inappropriateness, that's *ridiculous* coming from her. Mom has been wearing HIGHLY inappropriate halter tops and miniskirts purchased from Macy's Juniors department since her fiftieth birthday last month. Hello Irony, meet Hypocrisy. She won't even let me dye a streak of my hair blue. What's the ish? I already have blue braces and blue glitter fingernail polish.

"Thanks for *not* getting me something at Forever 21, by the way." I shoot the ball over her head, making her duck.

"I looked, but I wasn't sure what you'd like."

"I like jeans." I balance the ball on my finger like a Harlem Globetrotter. "They have to be the right shade of blue—not too light, not too dark."

"I like you better in skirts," Mom says. I don't answer her, busy with my ball. "Why don't you come

15

with me and we'll pick out some skirts together? Or jeans. We'll make a fun day of it."

Mom has clearly forgotten that we always argue in stores, because she never lets me get what I want. "No thanks." Mom's face falls. I don't know why. She doesn't need me to shop.

Swoosh. Another perfect shot. This time Mom sees it and smiles. I wait for her to say "nice shot" or "way to go." Instead, she says, "Drew, did you get that on film? We need fun family scenes to send to the videographer for your bar mitzvah video."

The garage phone rings.

Finsecker!!! No!

"I'LL GET IT!" I scream. I drop my ball, race past Drew, trip over my ball, bump into Mom, who drops her mail, and land on my butt.

"Abby!" Mom shouts. "Watch where you're going!"

I scramble back up, sprint to the phone, and yank it off the wall. "Hello?"

"Hello, this is Mr. Fartstinker calling to suspend you," says a fake deep voice.

I can't believe Caitlin. Why didn't she call me on my cell? She never calls our landline. "Yes?" I say, annoyed.

"I just saw Brett and his friends at Smoothie Hut, totally checking out Silent Amy. She was there with her mom. She looked really pretty. But you're prettier. I don't care what people say."

"You have the wrong number." I hang up. I know Amy is prettier than me. I don't need Caitlin to remind me. All the boys, including Brett, drool over Amy. They don't care that she's so basic all she does on the bus ride home is scroll through cat photos on her phone, not talking to anybody. What matters is that she has boobs, shimmery skin, the hottest clothes, and hair like Taylor Swift's. Then there's me, stick skinny with freckles and mosquito bites and dirty sneakers and the occasional chalk streak of blue hair. (Mom and Dad don't know about that last thing—they would go fully bonkers.)

Caitlin has been my best friend since third grade, but things aren't the same with us this year. She's been copying me a lot, and even though Mom says it's flattering when someone copies you, it feels competitive in a bad way. Caitlin tried out for Camp Star Lake because I did. As soon as I said I had a crush on Brett, she said she did too. She even started painting her fingernails the same color as mine, and everyone knows blue glitter nail polish is *my* thing.

Worse, she's been giving me compliments that are really put-downs. It started when Brett picked me for our duet acting project. Then when I got into Camp Star Lake, she said, "It's a lottery. Your audition has nothing to do with it." A total lie. She's also into punching me all of a sudden. I've told her to stop, but she keeps "forgetting."

The worst thing happened last week, when an avalanche of books and papers fell out of my locker. "Omigosh, Abby, you're such a *hoarder*!" she announced. Then Davis pointed and yelled, "HOARDER!" Not that I should care what Davis thinks. Yesterday he read, "The bride's face is covered with a veal," for his oral report. Still, even a weirdo calling you a hoarder isn't a good feeling.

Sometimes I don't even know why I'm still friends with Caitlin.

Actually, I do know why.

I don't have anyone else.

The truth is, I want to branch out from her and try hanging around with the kids from drama, or maybe the girls who were on my soccer team. But what if they don't want me? People already have their BFs and cliques. It's one thing to joke around in class or on the field with someone; it's another to make weekend plans with them.

The thing is, there's security in having a best friend. It's always been Caitlin and Abby, a unit. Caitlin says she's the only friend who will stick with me, because I talk too much, blurt out rude things, and cause chaos.

Maybe she's right. I don't know. What I do know is that people seem to like me once they get to know me. I always get picked first for teams in PE. But it's true that I talk and blurt and cause chaos, so she could be right.

Which is a downer, because I can't help being me.

Secretly, I'm glad Caitlin only made the alternate list for Star Lake. I'm looking forward to seeing what life will be like when I'm not one half of the Caitlin/Abby combo.

Mom interrupts my thoughts. "Grandma called. We're having dinner with her and Grandpa tonight."

"Ooh, are we eating at their condo?" Drew asks. He loves eating there because Grandma serves Jell-O as a side dish. I love eating there for three reasons: (1) Grandpa laughs like a maniac whenever I joke around, (2) he usually slips me some cash when it's time to leave, especially if I've scratched his back, and (3) Mom doesn't get on my case about every little thing I say or do because she's busy talking to Grandma. She even lets me eat the Jell-O side dish. I'm not allowed sugar at home, but I sneak it at every opportunity. I'm only human.

"Casa Lupita," Mom says. "Grandma has an early-bird coupon or something, I don't know."

"What's the occasion?" Drew asks, walking backward, pointing his camera at her.

"No occasion," she says.

Actually, the occasion is that I called Grandma and tipped her off about the coupon, which I saw in the *Clip N Save,* then reminded her I'm leaving soon for camp. Grandma said she misses me already and insisted on using the coupon. So now if Finsecker calls, we won't be home, which was my plan.

I am a genius. Earlier in the day I was an idiot. That's how it is with me.

I dribble the ball near Mom so I'm on camera too. "Is it no occasion that your favorite daughter will be away from the family nest for the first time? It's not all about Drew's bore mitzvah, you know."

"Stop calling it a *bore* mitzvah," Drew says. "My party will be awesome." He's talking about the dress-up banquet after his service. I've been to a few. The kids take off their shoes and rule the dance floor until the old ladies take over with a conga line. The whole shebang ends when the party favors come out, usually T-shirts printed with phrases like ELI'S HIP HOP BAR MITZVAH WAS THE SHIZZLE!

"Mike and Beth are coming tonight too," Mom adds.

Ugh. My other brother and his wife. Drew and I exchange disgusted glances. He turns the camera on himself and makes barfing motions. I drop the ball, grab my neck, and pretend to strangle myself.

Mom waves at Mrs. Kopecki walking her dog.

Drew aims the camera back at me. I fall on the driveway, spread-eagle, continue strangling myself until I gasp for air, choke, gurgle, and sputter, then add a few seconds of trembling and twitching for fake seizure purposes, until, finally, I roll my eyes upward, stick out my tongue, and die.

Mom steps over me and goes into the house.

4

To Drew and me, Mike is that red swollen thing on a baboon's butt.

At the restaurant, Grandma and Grandpa give me their standard greeting: "Hello, gorgeous!" Then they start arguing, also standard. "I don't like this place," Grandma says. "I never come here with my friends. It's so dark in here."

"So bring a flashlight," Grandpa shoots back.

"The service is terrible. Every time I come here it's terrible."

"I thought you said you never come here."

"We should have gone to Little Italy," Grandma says.

"Did you bring the coupon?"

"What do you think? Of course I brought the coupon. It's early, so you can still get a free drink at the bar."

That's all Grandpa needs to hear. He leaves the table and comes back two minutes later sipping a Manhattan. Mom recites the ingredients and Weight Watchers points of every salad on the menu. Dad shows me game scores on his phone, and Grandma suggests to the waiter that they turn the air-conditioning up.

Drew and I help ourselves to chips and salsa. He uses his spoon to catapult a chip into my mouth. It lands next to my eye. Drew dips another chip into the salsa so it's dripping. "Let's do that again. This time it'll look like you're bleeding. Ready?" He points the camera at me. "Action."

Dad yanks the chip out of his hand. "For Pete's sake, we're in a restaurant." "For Pete's sake" is Dad's favorite expression. Who is Pete, and why does Dad say things for his sake? I have no idea, but Dad likes to say it, or yell it when he's watching a football game, as in, "FOR PETE'S SAKE, WHAT KIND OF PLAY WAS THAT, YOU MORON?"

When I was in third grade, there was an article in a local magazine about how Dad left his career as "the most feared prosecutor in the state attorney's office" to follow his dream: owning a sporting-goods store. Mom and Dad always point out how his risky career choice paid off, because Dad makes way more money now than before.

"For Pete's sake, Mike and Beth are always late!" Dad half shouts to nobody in particular. Then he switches gears to cheerful mode, leaning in toward Drew with a grin. "So, how's my bar mitzvah boy?" Drew shrugs. He never has much to say to Dad.

"He's fabulous!" Mom answers for him. "He reads Hebrew like a rabbi. Oh, and I have to show you the RSVPs we got. Roz isn't coming."

Dad takes a corn chip and dips it in salsa. Mom shakes her head at him. She's been trying to get Dad to do Weight Watchers with her so he'll look good for the bar mitzvah, but his idea of dieting is going to the McDonald's drive-through and polishing off a Big Mac combo meal in his car, then throwing away the bag so Mom won't know about it.

"What about you, buddy?" Dad asks me, chewing. "How's school?"

I'm close to flunking English, there's a chance I'll get suspended, and I'm scared to death you'll get a phone call from my teacher tonight. "Outstanding." I kiss my fingers. "Simply fantastic, superb, and thank you so much for asking."

Dad pats his bald head with his napkin. The spicy salsa always makes him sweat. "Learn anything interesting?"

"We saw a movie in science today about face transplants," Drew offers.

"Gross," I say. "Do they take off the old face before they put the new one on? Or do they smoosh the new one over the old one? How does a person talk if they don't have their own lips?"

"Well, first they numb the guy's head, and—"

"So he's a numbskull," I interrupt.

"Can you let me talk for once?" Drew asks me.

I bow my head. "By all means. Please elaborate."

"Hey, now!" a deep voice booms out. My brother Mike.

Hooray.

Mom lights up like an arcade game. To her, Mike is Moses, all four Beatles, and Matt Damon rolled into one. To Drew and me, Mike is that red swollen thing on a baboon's butt. "Speaking of numbskulls," I whisper to Drew.

Mike's wife, Beth, is behind him, flicking her black hair with one hand, texting with the other. They look like celebrities, with their shiny suits and sunglasses perched on their heads. Beth is a vegetarian and works out a lot, and her rear end is on the larger side. She's glamorous, like a Kardashian, or maybe a broadcaster for Telemundo.

Mike works his way around the table, kissing Mom and Grandma. He turns to me next. "Hey, sis, when

are you gonna fill out? Just kiddin'. Looking good."
When he gets to Drew, he rubs his hand in Drew's
hair, messing it up. "*Duuuuude,* wassup? Got a girlfriend yet?" He laughs and points at Drew's I SPACED
OUT AT REUBEN'S NASA BAR MITZVAH shirt. "Time for some
new clothes, bro."

Drew fiddles with a button on his camera.

"So what was the giveaway for *your* bar mitzvah,
huh, Mike?" I ask him. "An *I think I'm Too Cool for
This Shirt* shirt?"

That takes the smirk off Mike's face. "I didn't give
out party favors at mine." Figures. He only thinks
of himself. Mike starts bragging about how he and
Beth joined the country club and went shopping for
a Lexus. Grandma goes, "Ooh, a Lexus," and moves
her penciled-on eyebrows up and down.

Dad listens to Mike, nodding along, and Mom is
so riveted it's like he's the only person in the room.
Mom tells him how proud she is that he and Beth are
doing so well with the real-estate agency they just
bought. Mike and Beth sell mansions to rich people.
Who cares?

Mike was Mom and Dad's only child for thirteen
years before Drew came along, and he is everything
Drew and I aren't. When Mike was in middle school,
he was on the lacrosse team and got straight As. In
high school he worked, and then he got a full scholar-

ship to college. Mr. Perfect Son. It's amazing Drew and I don't reflexively vomit at the sight of him.

The waiter comes, and we order. When it's Beth's turn, we all expect her to order one of her vegetarian usuals, like an all-veggie fajita. A ripple of shock goes around the table when she orders chicken tacos, same as me. "What, can't a person try something new?" she asks in this shaky voice.

Then, in one of those bizarre moments that usually only happen in movies, the whole restaurant quiets down, as if everyone in the room somehow knows a Big Announcement is coming.

Mom sucks in her breath. "Are you . . . expecting?"

Beth's usually rigid shoulders relax. "Yes, I'm twelve weeks along."

"Mazel tov!" Grandma shouts as Grandpa holds up his glass and whoops. My parents get up and hug and kiss Beth. They keep saying "Congratulations!" over and over. Then Mom and Dad kiss Mike, and then they kiss each other, for some reason.

A baby. Drew and I get up to kiss Beth on the cheek like everyone else is doing. After we go back to our seats, some ladies from another table come over to congratulate Beth. (Random strangers get personal all the time in Poco. Last week at Costco a woman pointed at the toilet paper in Mom's shopping cart and told her to switch to an unscented brand. They ended up discussing it for ten minutes.)

The restaurant is noisy again. Mom and Dad ask Beth a million questions about when did she know and were they trying (*ew*).

I can't imagine Beth's body getting all swollen, since she's such a fitness freak. "Beth, I can't wait to see you get fat," I say. I puff out my cheeks like a blowfish. "You're gonna get so huge, especially with your b—" I start to say *butt* and then stop myself.

It's too late. Beth stares at me, her expression going from disbelief to shock. Then her chin quivers as if she's about to cry.

And then she does cry.

I clap my hand over my mouth. Mike throws his napkin at me. "Do you ever think before you open your mouth, Blabby Abby? Oh, wait, don't try to think. You'll hurt yourself."

Everyone is looking at me like I just murdered a kitten.

5

That's the problem with unmentionables. I always mention them.

Our food arrives, but I don't feel like eating. Why can't I just be quiet, like Drew? Why do I always have to say every stupid thing that comes into my mind? "I'm sorry," I say over and over. I bet Mom's face will never light up for me the way it does for Mike. The expression she's giving me is the same one she has when she gets gum stuck to the bottom of her shoe.

Dad shakes his head at me. "For Pete's sake, Abby, you're not supposed to mention weight to a pregnant woman. Or any woman."

That's the problem with unmentionables. I always mention them.

"It's hurtful," Mom says.

"Very hurtful," echoes Grandma.

They're ganging up on me.

Beth sniffs, wipes her tears away, and straightens her shoulders. She looks like her regular self again. "It's okay. I realize children don't always mean things the way they sound." *Children*, she calls me.

"I didn't mean it to be hurtful," I say to Beth. "I just meant it'll be fun to see you pregnant, like, different from your normal self."

"Of course. It's fine." But it isn't.

"Okay, then," Mom says. "That's all Abby meant. Everybody forget about it." I know she's trying to help me, but it's obvious she's mad. She's cutting her chicken like she's sawing a tree.

Grandma reaches across the table to pat Beth's hand. "You know, honey, that's part of Abby's disease," she whispers. "The ABHB. She can't filter."

"ADHD, Ma," Mom says. "And it's not a disease. You don't have to whisper."

Grandpa goes, "What's the big deal? Pregnant women gain weight! This kid speaks her mind. She's going places. You'll all see." He winks at me. *I love you, Grandpa.*

"Beth." I don't realize words are coming out of me until I hear my voice. "I only meant that when you get humongous . . ." Beth winces at *humongous*. ". . . you know, right before you give birth, your baby could be the size of a Thanksgiving turkey . . ." Drew is waving his hand for me to stop. I can't. It's like a motor that won't turn off. "So your belly might look like . . ." I search for a word, search for a way out. ". . . like Dad's."

For a split second, nobody says anything. And then the tension snaps, like a twig. Dad laughs first, and everyone else follows. Even Beth manages a smile, especially when I rub Dad's stomach like he's a Buddha. After that, the grown-ups discuss which dead relative to name the baby after, and nobody cares that I hurt Beth's feelings.

Except me. I care. When I go to the ladies' room, Dad follows me and takes me aside. "I don't mind you using my belly for a joke tonight, but you shouldn't joke about it again, or anyone's weight, okay?"

I bury my face in his chest. "I'm sorry." He hugs me and kisses the top of my head. The thing about Dad is, he can be as loud and scary as an angry pit bull, but it passes quickly, and then he's a big mush ball.

After dinner I scratch Grandpa's back, and he slips me twenty bucks. He hugs me for a long time, as if he knows I need an extra-long hug today. Then he whispers in my ear, "You're my favorite grandchild. Don't tell the others."

I see him slip some cash to Drew and whisper in his ear. After that, he leaves with Grandma to go home and watch *Jeopardy!* Mike and Beth go home too, because Mike wants to read a bedtime story to Beth's stomach so the baby will know his voice, which is the stupidest thing I've ever heard, since I'm pretty sure the baby doesn't have ears yet. Dad, Drew, Mom, and I stay to have dessert.

On the way out Mom explains that she is too young to be called Grandma, so instead she wants to be called Glamma, like Goldie Hawn, whoever that is. "Isn't it wonderful?" she says to Dad as we go out through the glass door and onto the sidewalk. "First Drew's bar mitzvah, now the baby."

Dad puts his arm around her. "We have a lot to be thankful for."

I'm not so sure. Because standing right in front of us, about to walk through the restaurant's take-out door, is Mr. Finsecker.

6

I hate him infinity.

I hate Finsecker with every molecule of every cell in my body. I hate him from the roots of my hair to my intestines. I hate him infinity.

He drops the bomb as soon as he sees us. He really is going to suspend me. Worse, he tells my parents he expects me to fail the final.

Finsecker suggests my parents come to school for a meeting, but Dad insists the meeting take place right here in front of Casa Lupita, because he has a right to know what's going on with his daughter *now, for Pete's sake.* And when Dad uses that scary tone and does that furious jaw-twitching thing, people do what he says.

So while Drew waits in the car, Finsecker gives my parents his version of me. Apparently, I'm a troublemaker who can't string two sentences together, and I'm wasting my potential. I'm surprised he says I have potential. Teachers probably say that to ALL parents.

"Why didn't you let us know this was going on?" Dad asks, towering over Mr. Finsecker. "Isn't that your job?"

Finsecker seems to shrivel, but only for a second. "My job is to teach, Mr. Green. I have almost two hundred students. It would be impossible for me to contact the parents of every child who falls behind. It's your responsibility as parents to stay informed. All grades are posted online."

Mom never goes online to check my grades. "Why didn't *you* tell us, Abby?" she asks.

Tears spill out of my eyes and roll down my cheeks. How can I explain that Finsecker's class makes me feel like a passenger on the *Titanic,* doomed to sink, so why even try? How can I explain that I'm not like one of those *Titanic* passengers who looked for a lifeboat or asked a crew member for help, that I'm more like one of those musicians on the deck, the guys who kept smiling and playing violin and pretending everything was fine as the ship cracked in half?

How can I explain that if Mom and Dad had known

how bad it was, they would have pulled me out of *Grease* and off the soccer team, my only reasons for going to school? Or that I can tell when a teacher hates me, so I give back as good as I get, and trying my best for a creep like Finsecker is the *last* thing I would ever, EVER do? How can I explain that it started when I fell behind in three or four assignments because, even though I did them, I couldn't find them, then I felt lost in class, so cracking jokes was the only way to get through? How can I explain that I would rather have died than try to catch up and let people see how behind I was, and that redoing everything was frustrating and pointless since I'd already done it?

How can I even *begin* to explain?

"I—I—I don't know why" is all I can manage.

Finsecker says something about summer school. I'll be at camp, so that's impossible. I stop listening and count to ten in my head, tell myself that getting a suspension and bad grades in one class isn't the end of the world. *One, two, three, four . . .* "Self-talk," it's called. My doctor tells me to do it whenever I get angry or upset, so I can control it before it starts boiling and building inside me like lava in a volcano. *Breathe in, breathe out.*

"We'd better go," Dad says. He's calm now, his anger having vanished as quickly as it arrived. Finsecker shuffles into the restaurant.

35

When we get in the car, I finally talk. "Finsecker *hates* me. If schools really cared about bullies, they'd get rid of half the teachers."

Mom twists from the front seat and takes a long look at me. "You should have told us. I'm upset at you for lying, more than anything. How can we ever trust you again?" She turns around to face the front. "I'm disappointed in you." Dad nods.

That hurts so much more than if they had yelled at me. My parents will never understand. I start crying all over again.

"We can get our deposit back from that camp, right?" Dad asks Mom.

"What?! No!" I shout.

"I think so," Mom answers softly, as if I haven't yelled. "I'll call them tomorrow."

NO! "You promised I could go!" I say. "You promised! You can't do this!"

"You did this to yourself, Abby," Dad says. "You're going to summer school."

"No! You can't!"

But I know they can, and will. I beg, plead. Drew takes my side. It doesn't change their minds. I'm not going to Star Lake anymore.

Just like that.

7

You have, like, the worst luck ever.

When we get home, I slam my bedroom door, call Caitlin, and tell her what happened.

"I can't believe Finsecker was at the same restaurant. You have, like, the worst luck ever," she says.

"I'm not going to camp now. *Summer school*. It's so *unfair*."

"I didn't know they even *had* school in the summer. I mean, I've heard of taking make-up classes online, but forcing you to go to school over vacation? What a rip-off. They are stealing your youth, Abs. Seriously."

"It's all Finsecker's fault!"

"You know what would make you feel better? Revenge."

"Revenge? How?"

"I don't know. But I *do* know where he lives. Near Taylor, behind the mall. She told me he waters his yard with a hose. Not sprinklers. A hose. Psycho."

"What?"

"I'm telling you, you should get revenge. Don't get mad, get even."

It sounds like she's reading lines from a play. She doesn't understand that this is *real*, and it's happening to me. I hang up, then crawl into bed. Tears and snot ooze onto my pillow.

My phone beeps.

Hey Abby, Brett.

A text from Brett! He's never texted me before.

Brett: Have U started packing ur duffel 4 camp? I'm sneaking candy in bottom of tissue box how bout u? R u packing gum/ candy?

My duffel has been packed for a month, and yes, I packed Juicy Fruit gum in an empty shampoo bottle. Now I'll have to unpack everything, because I'm stuck here. I read his text again and again.

I can't go to Star Lake.

The more I think about it, the angrier I get. I keep going over everything that happened today, how Finsecker made fun of me, how he said something to me about horse manure, how kids whispered "sorry" when I walked out, trying not to cry. My anger builds faster and faster, like a car gaining speed down a steep hill. It twists and turns and spirals down my chest and crashes into my stomach. The next thing I know, I'm tossing my books and papers off my desk. Then I accidentally trip over my duffel bag, which makes me even madder, so I unzip it and throw everything I touch: clothes, sneakers, and flip-flops. I yell every bad word I know. I'm sure my parents can hear it all, but they still don't come in.

Now I'm pacing, my fists clenching and unclench-ing.

One . . . two . . . three. Calm down, Abby. Breathe. Four . . . five . . . six . . .

I HATE Finsecker! I want to put my fist through the wall, or break something. I throw my cell phone. Hard. It hits the wall with a *thump,* leaving a mark. I pick it up. The glass is cracked.

Shattered. Just like how I feel inside. The glass costs sixty-eight dollars to fix. I know the price because I've already dropped my phone and broken the screen three times. I have no birthday money left to pay for it. I'm so *stupid*.

The door flies open. Mom rushes in with Dad right behind her. "Abby! What was that noise?"

"For Pete's sake, this room looks like a tornado hit it."

My voice cracks. "I threw my phone."

"You broke the glass on your phone again?" Mom asks. Her lips disappear into a thin line. "You need to clean up this mess." Her voice is quiet but intense. She leaves.

Dad stays in the doorway. "You and I, we're going to have a talk later, buddy." After the door closes behind him, I hear Dad say to Mom, "She's too emotional to have a rational conversation right now."

"Don't you think I know that?" she answers.

"What are we going to do about it?"

Their voices fade away, and I can't hear the rest. I hate it when they talk about me like that, like they're detectives and I'm a case to be solved.

The crack in my phone looks like a jagged mouth laughing at me. How *did* this happen? How was everything so normal just a few hours ago, and now I'm flunking English, getting suspended, and going to summer school?

I pace back and forth, back and forth.

The urge to throw, break, or kick is still there.

Mom and Dad aren't even trying to see my point of view. Not even Caitlin understands the way I feel.

Caitlin. *Don't get mad, get even.*

I have an idea.

So what if I get caught? What will my parents do? The worst has already happened.

Three thoughts keep running through my brain, loudly:

IT'S NOT FAIR.

HE DESERVES IT.

I HAVE NOTHING TO LOSE.

8

We are in deep, serious doody.

I tiptoe downstairs.

"All you had to do was go online and check her grades," Dad says from inside his study.

"Why didn't *you* check?" Mom snaps.

I'll be back in an hour. They won't notice I'm gone.

It's so easy. I slip into the garage, get on my bike, and head out the side door. Caitlin and I meet up on the bike path. She has markers in her string bag, I have toilet paper in mine.

It gives me the heebie-jeebies, riding my bike at night, brushing past dragonflies while tree branches stretch out like long, bony arms. I'm going so fast my hair flaps behind me like a flag. "Slow down!" Caitlin calls. But I pedal like a speeding train, in time with my silent chant: *HedeservesitHedeservesitHedeservesit.*

Finsecker's neighborhood isn't far. We use the navigation app on Caitlin's phone and find his house, his car. Easy. No one outside. We work quickly.

First, we throw toilet paper into his trees, watching the long white strips stream down from the branches. After that we decorate his car. I draw caricatures of Finsecker's craggy face on one door while Caitlin draws devils on the other. I wonder if he'll have time to get to the car wash before school starts in the morning, or if he'll be late tomorrow.

"We have a problem," Caitlin whispers.

"What?" I loud-whisper back, adding hairy ears to my picture.

Caitlin walks to the street, dips the bottom of her T-shirt in a puddle, comes back to the car, and rubs the wet corner of her T-shirt on her drawing. "Look. It won't come off." She rubs harder. She sounds nervous. "I wanted to take off the devil horns, but they won't even fade."

"So cross them out."

"You don't understand." She picks up the marker

and turns it slowly, reading the fine print. "Oh. My. God." She hands it to me. "Look!"

I read it. *WARNING! Permanent ink. For window use only. Not for use on vehicle body.*

Our artwork is permanent. As in never coming off.

I can't think. I stare at Caitlin, my mouth in the same O shape of horror as hers.

"What are we gonna do?" Caitlin asks me.

"How should I know?" I ask, panic rising. "This was all your idea."

"No, it wasn't."

"Yes, it was!"

She puts her hand over my mouth. "Shhhh!"

I peel her hand off. "You said I should get revenge on Finsecker! You got the markers!"

"You called me to come out here!"

Bright headlights flood our masterpiece with light. The Neighborhood Watch car.

"Oh, no," moans Caitlin.

Two men get out. My heart thumps and bangs like loose change clanging in a clothes dryer. The marker falls out of my trembling fingers and rolls onto the grass.

Mr. Finsecker comes out in a plaid bathrobe and slippers. He looks different than at school: frail, old. Small. For a split second, I think it's Grandpa.

But it's Finsecker, all right.

He's standing in his driveway.

44

Which is *across the street* from the one *we* are standing in.

Meaning we aren't at his house.

Meaning the car we just trashed isn't his.

Meaning we are in deep, serious doody.

At the precise second this realization hits me, we're suddenly bathed in outdoor lights, and a hairy man in white underpants runs onto the driveway—the one we *are* standing on—waving a baseball bat.

"What did you kids do to my car?!" he screams. He steps closer, and it's clear he sees exactly what we've done to his car, because he makes this big gasping noise, and then yells: "ARE YOU CRAZY? YOU KIDS ARE GOING TO PAY FOR THIS! DO YOU HEAR ME?" He points his bat at the Neighborhood Watch men. "CALL THE COPS! I'M PRESSING CHARGES!"

Caitlin chooses this moment to throw up.

The squad car shows up almost instantly, lights flashing. Caitlin is sobbing. I'm shaking, but I manage to answer the officers' questions, at least until my parents drive up. Finsecker called them. I burst into tears as soon as I see their faces.

I've never been in trouble like this before.

Suddenly, I don't care about not going to camp anymore.

I'm more concerned about not getting arrested.

This is the worst thing I've ever done. I went too far, and there is no way out.

All the drama has left me exhausted. The police and Dad talked Underwear Bat Man out of pressing charges. Hello, we're twelve. We messed up his Ford Fiesta. We didn't murder anybody.

Instead of getting arrested, Caitlin and I have to pay $2,000 for a new paint job. Dad says I'll have to work at his store to pay him back. I also have to start my eighth-grade community service hours early by volunteering at Millennium Lakes Home for the Aged. It turns out Underwear Bat Man, also known as Mr. Aldo Meyers, is on the board there.

Will the glamour never end?

I wonder if I'll ever stop being a disappointment to my parents, if they'll ever look at me the way they look at Mike.

From now on, this will be known as The Night That Ruined My Life, or TNTRML.

9

It is beyond unfair.

It's been a week since TNTRML. The morning after it happened, Mom and Dad wanted to take me to Dr. Botwin, my ADHD doc, to discuss "my recent chain of poor decisions." I reminded them that the last time I saw her, she interrupted me to ask where I got my shoes. Dr. Botwin is possibly more ADHD than me. So now I have an upcoming appointment with some new doc. I'm due for my three-month checkup anyway.

Caitlin and I are Palm Middle's end-of-the-year headlining gossip story. The rumor is that we were arrested and have to go to juvie. I'm almost glad

Finsecker went through with the suspension, so I don't have to face people.

But I have to go back for finals. Classmates who used to say hi pretend they don't see me. I've never run with the popular pack, but I've always been cool enough to say hi to. Not anymore. Mom says they're ignoring me because kids sometimes just act that way in middle school, and I shouldn't let it bother me. I know better. They've decided I'm one of the bad kids who skip classes and hang around with high schoolers at the gas station.

Mom and Dad hired Aaron Kopecki to tutor me in English for my final. It didn't work. Even though I got As in math, drama, PE, science, and history, plus a B+ in Spanish (I could have gotten an A but didn't know Señora Blum took points off every time I shouted, "Ay, Chihuahua!" whenever she announced a *stupido* pop quiz), Finsecker gave me an F on my final. Shocker.

I've been begging Mom and Dad to let me make up English online, but Dad says his tax dollars pay for the summer-school program in our area, and I need to interact with a real teacher, for Pete's sake. They seem to forget Finsecker was a real teacher. A real *bad* teacher.

Did I mention I'm grounded? A prisoner in my own home, like those freaky pale girls in the movie *Mama*. Two days after TNTRML, THIS is what I found hanging on my bedroom door:

1) Laptop must be kept *out of your room*. Computer to be used only for homework. No social media.
2) No Netflix.
3) Homework must be done before you may go outside.
4) You cannot make plans unless you check with us first.
5) 9 p.m. bedtime, lights out, even on weekends.
6) Any violations will result in extra chores around the house, like polishing silver, washing the car, or emptying junk drawers.

I know I need to be punished, but this is *highly* overboard. No Netflix? *Nine o'clock* bedtime on *weekends*?

Drew laughs his head off. "Relax, there's no way Mom and Dad will enforce all of this." He takes a picture of the list with his phone. "My new screen saver," he explains. I crumple up the list and throw it at him.

"It's not a punishment," Mom tells me later. "We feel this will help you to form new habits." And then the kicker: "We're doing this because we love you."
!!

But out of everything that's gone wrong, THIS is the lemon juice on the paper cut that is my life: Caitlin gets to go to camp now. Since I'm not going, my spot at Star Lake opened up. Caitlin was an alternate. She got *my* spot. MINE. Every time I think about it, a silent scream goes off in my head.

Caitlin's parents are letting her go, even after everything that's happened. So Caitlin, who only tried out for Star Lake because I did, who vandalized that car the same as me, is now having the dream summer I was supposed to have.

It is beyond unfair.

10

Where are the delinquents?

I've never felt so small in my life. Beachwood Middle is gigantic compared to Palm Middle. Nobody is here yet. I made Mom bring me early so I'd have extra time to find my classroom.

What if I get lost? What if the teacher is strict and mean, like Finsecker? He or she probably will be, because who would want to teach summer school except someone miserable with nothing else to do? What if I fail again?

What if the kids are serious outlaws? I may have flunked a class and snuck out of my house to vandalize, but that was a one-time thing. *These* kids probably do stuff like that all the time.

Worst of all, what if I don't make a friend all summer? I'll be an outcast. I miss Caitlin. She might not win the BF award, but I don't face anything alone when she's around.

My meds don't work the way they're supposed to when I'm anxious. I calm myself down by reminding myself that summer school only lasts half a day, so I'll get to leave at lunch time. *You can do this, Abby. One . . . two . . . three . . . breathe.*

I find my room. It's empty. A sign reads ENGLISH/ LANGUAGE ARTS 7, MR. ANTHONY NORTON. There are no desks, just rectangular tables. I sit at one. The door opens, and an African American man holding a Starbucks coffee cup walks in. I recognize him. He taught at my school last year. He's young, early twenties.

"Hi there!" he says. "I thought I'd be the first one here." He drops his backpack on the floor and his coffee cup on a table and rubs his hands together like he's warming them over a fire. "Bright and early, I love it. You are?"

"Abby Green."

He smiles like I just gave him the best news in the world. "So *you're* Abby Green. Great to meet you! I'm Tony Norton." He holds his hand out, so I shake it. Since when do teachers shake hands with their students?

"You know who I am, Mr. Norton?"

"I've seen all my students' files, yes. And call me Tony."

What kind of teacher lets you call him by his first name? Is he the kind that's going to try to be our friend, or what? Tony starts dragging all the tables and chairs out of their rows, arranging them in a big circle.

"Can I help?" I always volunteer to put up bulletin boards or move things around. I need to get out of my seat often, and I love helping.

"Sure!" he says. If Tony is making us sit in a circle, maybe he's one of those touchy-feely teachers who always wants to talk about what a character is feeling, and what we're feeling reading about that character's feelings.

"Can I help you with anything else?" I ask when we're done.

"*May* you, not *can* you, and no, but thank you." He sips his coffee. "Any questions before the others get here?"

"Um . . . don't you teach at Palm Middle?"

"I subbed, but I'll be full-time this year." His grin fades. "Listen, Abby, I want you to know I've seen your IEP. I spoke to Mr. Finsecker about you." The mention of Finsecker has the same nauseating effect on me as a sudden drop on an airplane. "Seems he's left Palm Middle, by the way."

I throw my hands up as if my team just scored. "YES! I'll never have to see his face again!" Tony's expression tells me my outburst is inappropriate. "Sorry. Why is he leaving?"

"He got a job at Flaglin Community College. He always wanted to teach adults."

Maybe that's why Finsecker was always so harsh. He didn't want to teach kids.

"If it makes you feel any better, you're not the only student he failed," Tony says.

"Who else?" It's probably Davis. He has the IQ of a gnat.

"You'll see." Tony tosses his empty coffee cup into the wastebasket.

I clap. "Nice shot! What did Mr. Finsecker tell you about me?"

Tony pulls a notebook out, flips it open, and scans the page. "He says your reading comprehension is excellent, but your writing assignments are often incomplete." He bends his head down, reading. I lean forward and peek.

Irresponsible. Chronically disorganized. Disruptive. Unfocused.

Every word is a punch in the stomach. To Finsecker, I'm a list of wrongs, nothing but trouble. A zero.

"He also said you have a knack for decorating cars," Tony says with a slight smile.

I clamp my teeth together, forming a close-lipped wall of a grin. So this new teacher knows about TN-TRML. Great. "Well, at least my reading comprehension is excellent. I've got that going for me."

"Listen, what Mr. Finsecker didn't mention is that you're gifted in math and science. A lot of people with ADHD are gifted. 'Twice exceptional,' it's called."

"Yeah, my mom says Einstein had ADHD and was gifted. I tell her not to get her hopes up."

His laugh is warm and big. "Listen, I want you to forget about last year. My class is a fresh start for you, okay?"

Why is he being so nice? I didn't expect that. It makes tears well up in my eyes. I blink them back, take a breath, and say, "Fresh start. That sounds good."

Three Latina girls walk in, chatting in Spanish. They look normal—shorts, sandals, ponytails, not exactly the bad girls' club I was expecting. More kids arrive. They look okay too. An African American guy in a Miami Heat T-shirt; a tan surfer-type guy; a pale, freckled boy in cargo shorts with gelled hair. Where are the delinquents?

Tony is trying to be Mr. Friendly, asking them questions, but they give short answers. I feel sorry for him. Eventually, he stops greeting every kid and starts writing notes on the board, a list of class rules and some honor-code pledge. No one sits next to me.

Until I see a familiar pair of monkey pajama pants walking through the door.

11

Performers like me are always misunderstood.

Of course Trina Vargas would be the other student Finsecker flunked! Trina's grades are hardly refrigerator worthy. I'm so happy to see someone I know. Judging from the grin on her face, she feels the same way. She sits in the seat to my right, kicks off her flip-flops, rests her bare feet on the edge of the chair, and looks at me. Her leaf-shaped eyes stand out against her smooth, brown skin.

The sound of a police siren wails outside, then fades as it drives past the school. "Hear that?" Trina whispers to me, still grinning. "Your ride is here."

I don't know whether to tell her to step off or to laugh. I decide to laugh. "I didn't know you'd be here."

"Neither did I." She twirls a strand of her long, black hair. "The universe is, like, always surprising us with a new path."

Before I have a chance to ask her what the universe has to do with summer school, we both see him, standing in the doorway like a lost giraffe, wearing a striped T-shirt and shorts with a laptop tucked under his arm.

Magic Max failed? How the heck did that happen? Whenever Finsecker called on him, he knew the answer. After his initial look of surprise at seeing Trina and me, Max sits in the seat to my left, stretches out his long legs, and flips open his laptop. "Hi. I knew you weren't in juvie." His eyebrows knit together. "Is juvie even a real thing?"

"Yeah," I answer. "I saw a movie about it where Whoopi Goldberg took all these teenage criminals out for ice cream. Actually, it might have been a mental hospital, not juvie. One girl hid chicken bones under her bed. Whatever."

"At least they had field trips for ice cream," Max says. "Maybe we should have gone there instead of here."

Trina smiles. "You'd never last in juvie, Abby. You're too cute."

"Do you think I'm cute, Max?" I ask him, suddenly in the mood to joke around. "Do you?"

"Um . . . I don't know." His eyes stay glued to his laptop. "This site says there are one thousand, five hundred and eighty students attending summer school in Poco right now."

"Thank you, Captain Trivia," I say. "Let's get back to my cuteness."

"Yeah, answer the question," Trina says. "Do you think Abby's cute?"

Max keeps his eyes on his laptop. His cheeks and ears turn slightly pink.

"Are you *blushing*?" I ask him.

Trina laughs. "He is."

"Anything you three want to share?" Tony asks us. The whole class turns their heads in our direction.

Trina's eyes dare me to mess around. The words come out before I can stop them. "Max thinks I'm cute," I announce.

Trina goes, "Oh, no, you didn't!" and giggles. A few others, like the ponytail girls, look over and smile. I'm center stage, so I make the most of it. "Max, I've told you I don't like you that way! We're just friends!" Then I start copying the board, pretending I don't hear the soft laughter around me.

Max shakes his head like a dog with wet ears. "It's not true."

"So you don't think I'm cute?!" I shout.

He opens and closes his mouth, flustered. "I do. I mean, I don't. I don't know."

"Oh, yeah?" I ask. "Why is your face so red, then? You look like Clifford the Big Red Dog." People crack up big-time. Even Tony smiles. I keep going. "Seriously, dude, you look like a thermometer."

"Good metaphor, Abby," Trina says. "Respect."

"It's a simile," Tony corrects her. "That's enough, now."

"I think you're cute!" says the Miami Heat T-shirt guy. "And monkey pants too!" Trina and I look at each other and laugh.

"Kelvin, settle down," Tony says to him. "You'll have time to talk about who's cute after class." He goes back to writing on the board.

Max slinks down behind his laptop screen.

"You know I was just kidding, right?" I whisper to him. He doesn't answer, just types, looks up at the board, types some more.

I hate being ignored.

"So, like, what is the deal with your hair?" I ask. No answer. "Seriously, how do you avoid frizz and get your waves so shiny and manageable? Is it one of your magic tricks?" Still nothing but a dirty look. I lean toward Trina and whisper, "Magic Max is ignoring me."

She's ignoring me too, doodling a goblin with a

twisted mouth. I may live in my head sometimes, but I answer people when they talk to me. Everyone else is copying the board.

I start writing. I bet I'm way behind everyone else except Trina, who hasn't written a single word. Don't teachers know whenever we have to take notes only a few kids actually take them? The rest of us just copy later from the kids who took them.

Need. To. Focus.

This is so boring. When is Tony going to start talking? Max is typing away, probably posting something on a magician site. "So, Max," I say, "why are you in summer school?"

"Can you stop fidgeting with your foot?" he says. "You're shaking the whole table."

I stop. "Sorry."

Max looks past me at Trina. "Doesn't that shaking bug you?"

She holds up a drawing of a griffin. "It's giving my lines a freaky look, so I kind of like it."

I crack up.

"Well, I don't," Max says.

"Well, I don't like how you don't answer questions," I say.

Max folds his laptop shut with a loud click. "I don't like how you embarrass me in front of the whole class."

"I told you I was kidding!"

Max maneuvers his long, lanky self out from behind the table, takes his backpack and laptop, and goes across the room to sit next to Kelvin. "Don't go," I tell him. "Come on, don't be so sensitive."

Now I've bugged him so much I've made him leave. Performers like me are always misunderstood. But it bothers me when someone doesn't like me.

The door opens. My eyes almost pop out. I *cannot believe* who is walking in a half hour late and sitting next to me.

What in the name of Trina's monkey pants is Silent Amy doing here?

12

I should be the bagel.

After school I race upstairs, flop on my bed, and call Caitlin at Star Lake. Campers aren't supposed to have phones, but they sneak them in. I tell her about Finsecker leaving, about Trina and Magic Max and, of course, Silent Amy. "Little Miss Perfect has to go to summer school!" I sing. "Who knew? I thought she was an A student. You know, her face isn't that great if you really look."

"Yeah, it's her body that's amazing. Unlike you, she has boobs." Sadly true. My bras are so small, they get lost in the dryer like socks. "She's, like, perfect. I bet you anything her parents named their boutique

Teen Princess after her." Makes sense. Silent Amy *is* kind of a princess. She doesn't talk to us common folk. "So, what's it like being with that freak-fest Trina all day?"

I wince at *freak-fest*. "She's just spacey."

"Spacier than you?"

"Way spacier than me. But nice. The mute and the magician are another story. At least Trina's funny. They're all wackos, though."

"Trina's funny-strange. You know she's a genius, right?"

I snort. "Genius at what? Doodling goblins?"

"She invented an app that catches hackers. Brett said Microsoft wants to buy it."

I sit up. *Brett never talked to Caitlin before.*

"What about Magic Max?" Caitlin asks. "Why is he in dummy school?" I wince again. Does she have to call it that? "He's outer limits, even if he did save your butt in Finsecker's class after you almost took his eye out with your pencil."

I have a flashback of Max storming off to sit across the room. "He's a wet sandwich."

"You mean wet blanket, Einstein."

Max pops into my mind again, blushing because I embarrassed him. "He complained because I was shaking the table with my foot."

"You're shaking your foot now."

"How do you know? You're not even *here*." I hope she catches the resentment in my voice.

"I hear your headboard hitting the wall. You shake the whole bed when I sleep over." I stop wiggling my foot. "So guess what? I'm auditioning for this drama showcase with a monologue. Barbra Streisand did it in the movie *Funny Girl*."

"Who's Barbra Streisand?" I know who Barbra Streisand is. She was the grandmother in all those *Meet the Fockers* movies. But I won't give Caitlin the satisfaction.

"Abby, seriously? Barbra Streisand is only the most famous singer and actress ever."

"She can't be that famous if I've never heard of her."

"Google her. The monologue is 'I'm a Bagel.'"

I don't want to hear about it. *I'm* the funny girl, not Caitlin. I should be the bagel.

"Abby!" Mom calls from downstairs. "Ten minutes until we leave for your doctor's appointment!"

I hear a girl call Caitlin's name in the background. "I gotta go. You want to hear the best prank ever? We're putting grape Kool-Aid in our counselor's shampoo. It's going to dye her hair! Text me, okay? I'll get your mind off those losers you're stuck with."

We say our good-byes, and I hang up without telling her to break a leg. *She* is having *my* adventure.

Dummy school . . . those losers you're stuck with.

I put my pillow over my head and scream. When I come up for air, there are soft, white feathers flying out from a small rip in the pillow seam. I tear the rip wider, pull out more feathers, spread them across my palm, and blow. They float away, fall across my bed. Cool. I tear the rip wider, blow feathers everywhere.

My door flies open. Like a tsunami, Mom rushes in. And gasps. Not a small gasp either. A seeing-a-dead-body, there's-a-tarantula-in-my-bed gasp. "What did you do to that pillow?"

"Nothing. Don't worry about it." I start stuffing the feathers back in.

"Why did you rip that?!"

"It was already ripped. Look, I'm fixing it." Not really. Feathers keep escaping.

She puts her hand on her forehead and closes her eyes. "Please come downstairs. Now. We're leaving."

SLAM.

I hate my life.

13

When she sneezes, does it ever shoot out like a ball at a batting cage?

Before my appointment starts, Mom speaks to the new doc in her office while I sit in the waiting room. Mom doesn't know what to do with me anymore. I know this because I overhear her saying, "I don't know what to do with her anymore." I can't hear much else through the door, except the word *incentives* a couple of times.

After a few minutes the doctor calls me in. Dr. Ann Marie Catalano has puffy, blow-dried hair striped with yellows and browns like a marble cake, chunky jewelry, and lots of makeup. She tells me to call her

Dr. C. Something about her eyes freaks me out. It's like she's looking at me, but she isn't.

Dr. C goes to get something, leaving Mom and me alone on her couch. "What's wrong with her eyes?" I whisper.

"I think the left one is a glass eye," Mom whispers back. "My roommate had one in college."

"A GLASS EYE?" I whisper-shout.

"Shhhhh!"

"But how is that possible?"

Mom can't answer, because Dr. C comes back in and sits at her desk. She talks to me, but all I hear is *Glasseyeglasseyeglasseyeglasseye.* Dr. C puts her elbows on her desk. "Are you listening, Abby?"

"What?"

"What's on your mind?" she says. "You can be honest." Yeah, right. Whenever you're honest with an adult, they get royally ticked off or start lecturing you about whatever you just told them.

"I was just, um, wondering how long this is going to take."

"Are you sure you don't have any other questions?"

"What? No, I don't have a question about your eye."

Oops.

Mom shifts in her seat, touches her earring, then points to a painting of a smiling cat. "Well, you have a good eye for art. I love Britto."

"Thanks, I love Britto too," Dr. C says. "So, here's

the thing. I have a glass eye." Mom raises her eyebrows at me pointedly, her sign for *I'm always right.* Later, she'll say it out loud, for sure. "I was in a car accident when I was seventeen," says Dr. C. "I flew through the windshield, and they had to replace my left eye. Do you have any questions about that before we continue?"

Well, yes, I have a lot of questions. Is the place where her eye used to be hard and bumpy like the inside of a walnut, or soft and shriveled like a prune? When she sneezes does it ever shoot out like a ball at a batting cage? Does it feel like a marble? Or is it more like a grape? Can she break it like a lightbulb? What I decide to ask is: "When you put on eyeliner and you accidentally poke your glass eye, does it hurt?"

"No. I can't feel it at all."

I nod, indicating that I'm done, but add, "It's very pretty. It matches your other eye exactly."

"That's very sweet, thank you."

"I also like your hair," I tell her.

"Thank you," she says, running her fingers through her bangs.

"You could be a fashion stylist," I add. "For women your age. Not for teens."

Mom gives me her *stop talking* look. "Why don't we get started?" she says.

"Okay," says Dr. C, opening her laptop. She puts on

purple reading glasses with rhinestones, types a little, then looks at me. "So, Abby, your mom explained why you're in summer school, but I want to hear it from you. How do you think you got to this point?"

I don't have an answer. I don't know why or how I get to any point.

"Do you know what an impulse is, Abby?" Of course I know what an impulse is. She tells me anyway. "It's a sudden, strong urge to do something without thought." *Duh.* Dr. C shifts her attention to Mom. "Did you know there was a problem with Abby's English grades?"

"No." Mom fidgets with her purse strap. "I've been pretty hands-off. Abby's grades were excellent in her other classes, so I never guessed there was a problem in English."

Hands-off? How about *whole body* off? If Mom was honest, she'd admit she's been putting me on hold these past few months because she's been OBSESSED with Drew's bar mitzvah, plus her fiftieth birthday and everything but me.

"Look at what her drama teacher said." Mom pulls a booklet out of her purse. It's my program from *Grease.* I thought I'd lost it. "I brought this so you could see this side of Abby."

Dr. C opens the program and reads, "To the best Rizzo I've ever directed, you are an exceptional comedic actress. From your biggest fan, Mrs. A. Jenkins." Dr. C peers at Mom over her reading glasses. "You must be proud."

Mom takes the program back. "Abby is very talented."

She doesn't say she's proud.

Dr. C turns back to me. "So, tell me, since you're obviously intelligent and have a lot going for you, what do you think went wrong in Mr. Finsecker's class?"

"Well . . . I couldn't concentrate when he was teaching."

"Why not?"

"Because he's *slow* and boring and mean."

"What about keeping up with your work?"

I shrug. "What we were reading made no sense, at least not to me. I started skipping the reading, and then thinking I had more time for assignments when I didn't. . . ." I shrug again.

"And everything went downhill from there," Dr. C says, typing as I talk. "Time management was an issue."

"Yes. It also went downhill because Mr. Finsecker picked on me. Ask anybody."

Dr. C nods, listening. "That happens. I wish every teacher could be like your drama teacher, but the truth is that a lot of teachers don't have much knowledge about ADHD. It's terrible, but that's the way it is."

"It is terrible," I agree. I expect her to ask what I did in class that made Finsecker single me out, but she doesn't.

"Eye contact, Abby," Mom reminds me quietly. Sometimes I forget to look adults in the eye when I'm talking to them. I usually look at their lips. It dawns on me that Mom shouldn't have said "eye contact" in front of a lady with *one* eye. Mom must be realizing that right about now too, because she quickly goes, "Never mind."

"What about your behavior outside of class?" Dr. C asks me. "Do you have conversational accidents? Times when you say hurtful things to someone without meaning to?"

Hello, and welcome to the story of my life. "All the time," I say.

Dr. C stops typing. "I have a patient who says her mouth is like a bomb, and after it goes off, she's always cleaning up the damage."

"Yes! That's exactly what it's like."

Dr. C leans toward me. "Listen, your brain is working so fast that your mouth can't keep up with it. Having a fast brain is a *good* thing. It's part of what makes you so smart and talented. But it means you have to *slow down* in social situations. Stop and think about how a person will *feel* before you say out loud whatever pops into your head. Same thing goes for when you're angry or upset."

I've heard the "Think Before You Speak" speech before. It's right up there with "Be More Careful" and "Control Your Impulses." If all those things were so easy to do, I would have done them already.

There's only one thing that helps. "My meds slow me down. They help me stop my mouth, although I still say stuff I shouldn't once in a while," I tell her. "It's worse when I forget to take my medicine."

Mom explains, "I put her pill out and leave Post-it reminders for her, but she still forgets sometimes. She only takes it on school days, so she doesn't struggle with sitting in her seat and staying focused. On weekends, she doesn't take it at all, unless there's a lot of homework."

Dr. C types and talks. "It's your responsibility to remember, Abby. Do you ever forget to brush your teeth in the morning?" I shake my head no. "Then can you remember to take your pill?" I nod. "Good," Dr. C says. "Your mother has to get ready in the morning like you do. She can't watch you every second. You're old enough to find a system that works for you."

"I know that." No more babyish Post-its. I'll *prove* to Mom I can remember.

Mom looks worried.

Dr. C asks me more about Finsecker's class and school. She doesn't get that glazed look people sometimes get when I tell a long story. She talks about how I need to stop and think about what I'm feeling when my anger takes over, and compares it to hitting pause on a remote control, or slamming the brakes on my bike. Then we discuss managing my emotions, how I need to *respond,* not *react.* She says I can come in anytime I'm going through a rough patch or want to see her, that I don't need to wait for my three-month checkup, and asks if there's anything else I want to mention. I tell her about how I spend so much time saying I'm sorry to people, and I'm not very good at it.

"Why don't you start writing letters?" she suggests. "Sometimes writing a letter can be the best kind of apology, because you can get the words just right." Dr. C closes her laptop, laces her fingers together, and rests her chin on her hands. "Let me ask you something, Abby," Dr. C says. "How do you feel about the way things went down these last couple of months, or your new summer plans?"

How does she think I feel? "I'm not happy about it."

"So, then, are you interested in doing some work on yourself and making changes?"

I'm about to joke that "doing work on yourself" is what my grandma calls a face-lift, but Dr. C holds up her hand like a traffic officer. "Wait. Take your time before you answer me, because if you say yes, I'm going to hold you to it. *Think*."

I picture Beth crying because of what I said in the restaurant, and the looks on Mom's and Dad's faces when Finsecker was telling them about me on the sidewalk. I think about the car Caitlin and I ruined with devil pictures, about the mark on Magic Max's forehead when I accidentally hit him with my pen, and how I made him turn red in Tony's class.

I think of Mr. Finsecker on his driveway in his faded bathrobe.

"So?" Dr. C asks. "Are you willing to make changes?"

"Yes. I'm willing to make changes."

Mom and Dr. C share a meaningful look, like they've made a breakthrough.

A thick heaviness fills my chest. Because I know the truth. At the end of the day, I'll still be me, and that's not what they want.

❋

ROUGH DRAFT:

Dear Mr. Finsecker,

I am writing to you to apologize. I'm sorry I was ever put in your class with your mushroom-and-old-sofa-smelling self. I'm sorry my dad had to write a check to get your neighbor's car repainted, which I have to pay back by working at his store. I'm sorry I'm grounded, because staying indoors and doing nothing is a lot harder for me than it is for most people.

Did you know, Mr. Finsecker, that camp was the only bright, shining beacon of light at the end of the long, dark tunnel of horror known to you as school? Now that light is gone, thanks to you.

I almost puked when you told my parents it was a pity you didn't teach summer school, because if you had the opportunity to teach me all over again, I could start over with a *tabula rasa*. I don't know if a *tabula rasa* is a death threat or some kind of Mediterranean pita dip or what, but I do know that I'd rather kiss a rabid dog, clean a public toilet, see my grandpa in a Speedo, and go to juvie than have to sit through the torture that is your English class.

Please glue this note to your useless English book, or stick it in your giant hairy ear.

Love,

Abby Green

FINAL DRAFT:

Dear Mr. Finsecker,

I am writing to apologize for the pain and suffering I have caused you. I am sorry for not applying myself in your class, for being disrespectful, and for the car incident with your neighbor, Mr. Aldo Meyers. I deeply regret my actions. I will do my best to right my wrongs by doing community service and working hard in summer school.

Please accept my apology.

Sincerely,

Abby Green

✳

ROUGH DRAFT:

Dear Mr. Aldo,

My name is Abby Green, and I am writing to apologize for the unfortunate incident with your car. My friend Caitlin and I used poor judgment. Then again, you used poor judgment when you bought those tighty-whities. Nice underpants. Also, what kind of name is Aldo? That sounds like a dog food. And what kind of person swings a bat at kids? Do we look like terrorists? You're obviously mental. Thanks for making my cruddy summer even worse by forcing me to volunteer at your old-folks' home. Can't wait to hang with you and the fossils. I'll bring the Clay Aiken CDs, you bring the Activia. Later.

Love,

Abby Green

Dear Mr. Aldo Meyers,

  My name is Abby Green and I am writing to apologize for damaging your car. I used poor judgment, and for that, I am sorry. I look forward to volunteering at Millennium Lakes. Please accept my apology.

  Sincerely,

  Abby Green

Mom said I only have to write letters to Mr. Finsecker and Mr. Meyers.

  But there are a couple more I want to write.

TO: Beth@PocoRegalHomes.com
FROM: AbbaDabbaDoo@yahoo.com
SUBJECT: Apology

Hi Beth,

  I'm writing to you to apologize for saying I can't wait to see you get fat. I've been thinking about you a lot. Drew says my mouth is an early riser, but my brain sleeps in, which means I say things that come out wrong. I hope the baby looks like you and not Mike, because you're very pretty, no matter what weight you are.

  When the baby comes, I'll be happy to babysit for you, if you'll let me. For free, even. I hope you don't get sick and throw up a lot like Mrs. Jenkins did when she was pregnant. She barfed into the wastebasket in class. It was gross.

   Sorry again.

   Love,

   (Soon to be) Aunt Abby

PS When Mike said I need to fill out, that hurt my feelings too.

PPS If you decide not to name the baby after a dead relative, please consider the name Sabrina for a girl, or Brett if it's a boy.

14

Abby Cadabra.
(See how I turned my name
into a magic reference?
You're welcome.)

What Dr. C said about brushing my teeth helps me come up with a way to remember to take my medicine: I leave myself a giant note in my bathroom. It works. This morning, I make my breakfast, take my medicine, make my bed, and put away my laundry (throw it in the closet, same thing).

"It's a start, Abbles," Mom says. "Try to remember to put the milk away next time."

The milk. I always forget something.

Before I head out, I check my email. No reply from Beth. Fine. I don't want anything to do with her either. Maybe she didn't get my email? I could send her a text. No. She didn't accept my apology. Some things you can't undo. I try not to think about it, but I keep checking my email on the way to school.

When I get there, I spot Max in the hall, speed walking to avoid me like I have the bubonic plague (a gross infection from Shakespeare's day we learned about yesterday). I catch up to Max pretty quickly since I'm wearing sneakers and shorts today. "Max, wait up!" He turns around, and I hand him my note. "IwouldhavetextedyoubutIdon'thaveyournumber," I babble before taking off. I don't want to stand there while he reads it.

> Max, I didn't mean to upset you yesterday.
> I like to joke around. You may have noticed.
> I didn't think you'd get so angry. I thought you
> would laugh. You should sit with Trina, Amy,
> and me. We Palm Middlers are pretty much all
> we have this summer. We have to stick together.
> Come sit with us again.
>
> Abby Cadabra.
> (See how I turned my name into
> a magic reference? You're welcome.)

When I get to our room ahead of Max, I'm surprised our tables aren't in a big circle anymore. Then I remember that Tony and I rearranged them at the end of class yesterday, so now we're sitting in groups of four called quads. He also had me put an extra couple of tables in the back corners, facing the wall.

Tony set up my quad away from the window, since I get distracted watching cars go by outside. Amy and Trina sit with me, but Max doesn't. Instead, he pulls up a chair at another quad with four other boys. I guess my note had no effect on him whatsoever.

Tony takes one look at Max, says, "That's not going to work," picks up Max's laptop, and places it across from me. "Max, you're sitting here."

"Guess you'll have to talk to me now," I say to Max after he sits down. "Did you read my note?"

"Yeah." He doesn't look at me, just opens his laptop. This guy is as pleasant as a cramp.

"All right, listen up," Tony says. "We're all going to be spending a lot of time together, so I think we should get to know each other." Tony starts handing out papers. "Interview the person sitting opposite you using these questions." Great. I get Max, Mr. Personality. "This questionnaire isn't for a grade, but you'll be turning it in."

Papers swish and conversations buzz as people start interviewing each other. I fumble in my backpack for a pencil. I sharpened five the other night but can't find a single one. Typical. Max drums his fingers on his desk, waiting.

Trina and Amy have already started. "What do

you hope to achieve in this class?" Trina reads. Amy whispers something back. Trina puts her hand over her ear. "What?" Amy tries again. Trina sits back in her seat. "This isn't going to work. Why don't we answer these questions through interpretive dance?" She weaves her arms in and out. I join in, waving my arms. Trina and I get into it, cracking each other up. Amy laughs too, but no sound comes out. Max sits back and observes us like we're germs under his microscope.

"Hey, what's going on over there?" asks Tony.

We stop with the arm dancing.

I go back to hunting for a pencil. Amy is probably criticizing me in her head for being so disorganized, but then she surprises me, handing me a brand-new sharpened pencil. It's pink and sparkly. "Here," she whispers.

"Thank you," I say. Instead of responding, "You're welcome," she just gives me a blank smile and blinks. Bizarre. I appreciate the pretty pencil, though. I hope I don't lose it.

Now is my chance to win Max over. "Finsecker was excruciatingly boring, don't you think?"

"Yes." He reads from the paper. "How do you plan to achieve your academic goals?"

"By paying attention. I just paid attention to how the word *tingly* is in the word excrutia*tingly*."

Max writes that down as if it's a real answer. Not

even a hint of a smile. "Are you available for children's parties?" I ask. "Because you're a barrel of laughs."

"As a matter of fact, I *am* available for children's parties." He says this solemnly, the way a rabbi would say "I am available for funerals."

"What would you do at children's parties?"

"Magic shows."

"Oh."

"Question three. What are you good at, besides losing your pencils?"

"Losing my mind?" Trina and Amy overhear and giggle.

Max stares at me for a second, then says, "Making people laugh." He writes that down.

We're almost having a nice moment. "You should try laughing more, Max."

"What's there to laugh about? We're in summer school."

"Good point, but I'd rather laugh than be miserable," I tell him. "So relax and stop with the cold-fish act."

"It's not an act."

"You're a cold fish?" I ask. "Because I find you to be more of an anemone. Are you a friend or an anemone?"

Max shakes his head and sticks his long legs out to the side of the table.

"Wow, you have hairy legs!" I blurt out. "It's like

84

you're wearing furry khaki pants." His head snaps back. Trina and Amy laugh, then stop when they see his stung expression. "Sorry, was that mean?" I ask.

He stares at me. I don't know what he's thinking. "You can't tell when you're being mean?"

"Not always, no."

He scans my face, probably to see if I'm messing with him. "Well, yeah, that was a little mean."

"Then I'm sorry."

His face softens. He looks down at my legs. "Why do you have so many bruises? Do you have a disease?"

A big belly laugh bursts out of me. "The only disease I have is tripping or banging into things. Look." I stand up and point to the bruise on my knee. "I call this one the Finsecker, because it was his fault. What continent do you think it looks like?"

All three of them stare at it. Finally, Amy whispers, "Australia?"

"Right!" I sit down. "Max, tell her what she's won!"

"Abby, please stay in your seat," Tony says from his desk.

Max is sort of half smiling. I feel like he's finally warming a little. "Listen, you're not mad at me anymore, right?" I ask him. "Because, like I told you in my note, I said that stuff yesterday because I was bored. No big deal."

The half smile disappears. "No big deal? You made

fun of me in front of the whole class on the first day at a new school. You said I look like Clifford. You made fun of, like, the way I blush. Just now, you said I was a cold fish. News flash: All of that is mean. It's also *obnoxious*."

I hate that word. Only people with no sense of humor use it. As if reading my mind, Trina goes, "Abby's not obnoxious, Max. You've got to learn to take a joke."

"Yeah," Amy murmurs.

"One more minute, guys," Tony announces. Max and I have barely done anything. Neither have Trina and Amy. I'm not the only one with time-management problems around here.

"If I sit with you," Max says to me, "how will I know you won't embarrass me again?"

I put my hand over my heart. "I keep my promises, and I promise I won't make fun of you in public."

"What about making fun of me in private?"

"I might make jokes to your face. Or about your face. You'll just have to accept it."

Max squints at the ceiling as if there's an answer there. "Okay, I accept your apology."

I hold up my hand for a high five. "Good talk." Max slaps it. Trina and Amy do too; then they slap Max, and then each other. We're Team Palm Middle.

I feel better about things.

"Let's celebrate our reunion with more interpretive

dance!" I sway my arms side to side. Trina bends her elbows, Egyptian style. Even Amy moves a little bit. I didn't think she had it in her to loosen up.

Max looks away, pretending not to see us.

While Tony collects the questionnaires, I get to thinking. My biggest fear was not making a friend this summer. I look at Max, Trina, and Amy. I wonder if they had the same fear. We have nothing in common. But that's okay.

At least we have each other to talk to.

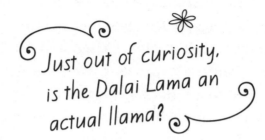

Just out of curiosity,
is the Dalai Lama an
actual llama?

I want to unzip my skin and jump through a portal to anywhere. GET ME OUT OF HERE.

It's Friday, almost time to go. This morning I woke up at the crack of dawn, starving, so I had breakfast and took my meds much earlier than usual.

Big mistake.

I waggle my pencil, chip off my nail polish, twirl my hair into knots. I'm not the only one twitching. Max is practicing a trick, hiding coins between his fingers. Sofia, the leader of the ponytail girls, is texting behind a stack of books on her desk. Trina is busy doodling centaurs, and Kelvin is peeling Miami Heat stickers off his notebook.

It's going to be a long summer.

I wonder what Caitlin is doing right now.

Focus, Abby. Pay attention.

Tony rubs his hands together. "Today you all get your first creative-writing project. Free choice. It can be a review, letter, article, or poem."

A chorus of groans and eye rolls is our class's response, with a sarcastic "wahoo!" from Kelvin. Tony raises his voice over ours. "The best part is, you don't have to write about Shakespeare!"

"I FEEL SO ALIVE!" I yell.

Tony doesn't get angry at Kelvin or me for Being Disruptive. "Okay, guys, settle down. Every quad will have a different topic, but each student will do the assignment on his or her own. Anyone have a subject they'd like to propose? It can be anything."

"Magic," Max says.

"The Dalai Lama," Trina suggests.

I'm not good at creative writing. Maybe he'll assign me something else. I raise my hand. Tony points at me. "Just out of curiosity, is the Dalai Lama an actual llama? Or a dolly?" I ask. "I mean, what *is* a llama? I've never been clear on that."

"Look it up, Abby," Tony says dryly. "Okay, more topics, people."

"Movies!" I shout.

"*Madden NFL,*" says Kelvin.

"Surfing!"

"UFOs!"

"Funny movies!" I put in. I could write about that. Probably.

"Guatemala," Sofia says.

"*Sí,* Guatemala," repeats one of her friends.

Silent Amy jots it all down as if we're getting tested.

"Transcendental meditation," says Trina. "Yoga. Art forms."

Tony pauses. "Art forms. Now, that has interesting possibilities."

I wish Tony had said my suggestion was interesting. "Comedies!" I shout again, *dying* for him to choose mine. "Movies and TV shows!"

"I heard you, Abby," Tony says. I wonder how long his niceness will last before he turns into the same kind of non-smiling teacher who put us all here. The enemy. He points at our quad. "You four will each choose an art form and write about it." Who cares about art, besides Trina? Everybody loves movies. The other quads get Guatemala, UFOs, and surfing.

"Are funny movies considered an art form?" I call out.

"Yes," Tony says. That's a relief. I'll do a movie review. "Give facts and opinions. Your thoughts are important to me."

"We don't have any thoughts," I say. "That's why we're in summer school."

Tony waits for the snickers and hooting to stop. "Abby, see me at dismissal." I knew his niceness wouldn't last. "Okay, people, finish act one of *A Midsummer Night's Dream*."

After class I go up to Tony's desk. He leans back, puts his hands behind his head. "I bet you think I've called you here to tell you to stop calling out, give you a warning, maybe some threats . . . right?" I nod. "Well, I didn't call you up here for that."

"Okay."

"What do you think would help you to control yourself during my lesson? Do you want to sit next to me? You're very verbal, so maybe I should move you to a different quad."

"NO!"

Tony's shoulders jump.

"Excuse me, I'm sorry," I say. "Please don't do that. I can do better. This time of day is bad, that's all. PLEASE don't move my seat."

"Okay, I won't. But you have to stop talking and get your work done if you want to stay. For smaller assignments, you can stay where you are, but for tests, let's move you to an extra table in back and see how it goes. There will be no distractions back there. Afterward, you can sit with your quad."

I dig my fingernails into my palms. "You won't put me in the hall, will you? I had a teacher who did that once." Mrs. Purcell, fifth grade. Kids and teachers stared at me on their way to the restroom. I couldn't focus at all. I felt like I had *stupid* written on my face.

"I would never put you in the hall," Tony assures me.

Phew. I feel tears building up. Tony understands. A lot of teachers don't. I swallow my pre-crying throat lump.

Tony waves his hand and leans back in his chair. "One more thing. Your questionnaire says you're good at making people laugh, and I agree. Have you ever thought of doing stand-up comedy?" he asks.

"What? No, I've never done anything like that." On YouTube there are videos of comedians getting verbally abused by audiences. People throw drinks at the stage. No thanks. "Why?"

"Because you do stand-up comedy every day, in my class. You simply do it from your seat, not a stage."

I've always thought of myself as a comedic actress, or possibly a TV personality/talk-show-host type. I'm not a stand-up comic. I shake my head. "I don't think so."

"Listen, Abby, I want all my students to make the most of their talents. So how about if I make you a deal? If you stop calling out and interrupting while I'm teaching, I'll pick a Friday and allot a few minutes at the end of the day, and you can come to the front of the room and showcase your talents. Tell stories, do characters, jokes, whatever. What do you think?"

What do I think? I think for once, a teacher is *rewarding* me for my big mouth instead of punishing me for it. "It's a deal. Thank you." I can't stop smiling. "Thank you," I repeat idiotically.

"You're welcome."

"In Shakespeare's day," Tony says, "two of the best-known stand-up comics were Lucretia the Tumbler and Jane the Fool."

"There were stand-up comics in old-timey England?"

"Yes, famous ones. They were called fools, but 'fool' wasn't an insult then. Being a fool was a profession, and some were women. The good ones became famous and performed for royalty. If they could do it then, you can do it now."

Can I? Maybe. Why *haven't* I tried stand-up comedy before?

TO: AbbaDabbaDoo@yahoo.com
FROM: Beth@PocoRegalHomes.com
SUBJECT: Re: Apology

Hi Abby,

Thanks for your email. It was very grown-up of you to write and apologize. I know you didn't mean to hurt my feelings. Sometimes we all say things we shouldn't. It's okay.

I want to share a secret with you. Besides my parents, only Mike and my best friend know this, and now you. When I was your age, I was so overweight, my parents sent me to a diet camp. I had to go every summer until I got my weight under control. Growing up, I couldn't wear the clothes other girls wore, and I never felt like going anywhere because I didn't like the way I looked or felt.

That's why I work out so much and watch what I eat. It's become a big part of my life, making sure I don't gain back the weight. So knowing I'm about to get fat all over again scares me and makes me sad, even though it's for the best reason in the whole world. That's why I cried so much at the restaurant. When you said you couldn't wait to see me get fat, it triggered something inside me from my past, and I cried. I hope you understand. I'm sorry if I made you feel bad.

I know sometimes it's hard for you to keep quiet, but this time, I know you'll keep my secret. It's a big one. I trust you. I also know you'll make a great aunt.

Thanks again.

Love,

Beth

PS I'll tell Mike not to make that comment to you anymore about filling out. Sometimes he says things he shouldn't, just like you.

PPS I like your baby-name suggestions. Mike and I will definitely add Brett and Sabrina to the list of options we're researching.

16

A grown-up has never apologized to me. Never.

I read Beth's email five times. I have no idea why she trusts *me*, "Blabby Abby," with keeping her secret, but I won't tell, not for a million dollars. A grown-up has never apologized to me. Never.

Mom's fork is poised in midair as she watches me stare at my dinner. "You're miles away."

"Huh? Oh, nothing." I push my chicken around.

Dad makes a face at the mystery mound on his plate. "For Pete's sake, Rachel, what is this, dirt?"

"It's quinoa," Mom answers. "Five Weight Watchers points."

Dad cocks his head toward Drew and me enjoying

our mashed potatoes. "How come *they* don't have to eat this?"

"They need calories. We don't." She forks quinoa into her mouth. "Eat your chicken, Abby. How's summer school?"

"Exhilarating. A dream come true. I love it. Thank you so much."

"What about day camp?" Dad asks Drew.

"Film camp," Drew corrects him. "Today we made blood from corn syrup and food coloring. We're shooting the stabbing scene tomorrow."

"How delightful," Mom says. "Make any new friends?"

"Yes," he answers. I know it's not true.

Drew and I never cough up friend info. Which details do Mom and Dad want? That the bully who called Drew and his friend Sameer "midget" and "armrest" last semester tossed their backpacks in the trash? That my supposed best friend calls me names and punches me? Or that I put up with it because I don't have another close friend? Parents always think they want details, but they're better off not knowing. That's the truth.

"I've been thinking," Dad says. *Oy.* Whenever Dad says he's been thinking, he comes up with a terrible idea. "How about a football theme for Drew's bar mitzvah reception? Every table could be a different team."

"What are you talking about?" Mom asks, her

voice rising. "I've already ordered centerpieces and T-shirts. The theme is movies!"

"Calm down, for Pete's sake. It was just a suggestion."

"I hate football," Drew says quietly. Or maybe he just seems quiet compared to my parents.

"Maybe you wouldn't hate it if you tried it," Dad says. "The next time Abby and I are tossing a football, you should—"

"Drew has hundreds of followers on YouTube for his short films," I butt in.

"Steven Spielberg got started with short films," Mom says. "So there you go."

"And I know for a fact he *never* played football," I declare with authority. I have no idea if Steven Spielberg played football or not.

Drew shoots me a grateful look. "My party theme was supposed to be *horror* movies, but forget about what *I* want for my own bar mitzvah."

"Andrew," Mom says, "I cannot have the rabbi and his wife sitting at the *Texas Chainsaw Massacre* table. They're sitting with us at the *Star Wars* table."

"Lame," I say. "I'd much rather sit at the *Texas Chainsaw Massacre* table." I pick up my knife and wave it around like an electric saw. *"Rrrrrrrrrrrrrrrrrr, rrrrrrrr, rrrrrrrrrrr. Aaaahhh, aaahhh!"*

Mom rubs her temple. "Abby, we're at the dinner

table." Wait for it. . . . Wait for it. . . . "This is not the Abby show." There it is. "Please put your leg down." I take my foot off my chair. I always forget I'm doing that.

"Did you come up with a system to help you remember to take your pill every morning?" Mom asks. "Like we talked about with Dr. C?"

"Yup," I answer. "I wrote TAKE YOUR MEDS on my bathroom mirror in lipstick. So I can't miss it when I'm brushing my teeth. Good idea, right?" Personally, I think it's brilliant.

Mom puts her fork down. "You used my lipstick? Without asking? Please tell me it wasn't the Chanel one. Was it the Chanel one?"

"I don't know. It was red." To change the subject, I slide the bowl of quinoa toward Drew. "Want some dirt? It looks delicious."

Drew sneeze-laughs, sending chunks of mashed potatoes shooting out of his mouth. A blob lands on Dad's chin.

Drew and I lose it laughing.

"Something funny, you two?" asks Dad. I'm about to say, "Yeah, it's snowing on your face," but Dad holds up his finger, warning me, "Watch your mouth."

"That's physically impossible," I giggle. "Unless you're standing in front of a mirror."

"Or using your phone cam," Drew adds.

"Or have unusually large lips," I say with a French accent.

I reach for the salt and accidentally knock over my water, then try to wipe it up with my napkin. Drew and I can't stop giggling.

The sight of Dad's face makes me go into hysterics. I jerk forward, doubling over in a wave of uncontrollable laughter, and *BAM*. My forehead hits the corner of the table.

I sit up, dazed. They're all staring at me, goggle-eyed. Drew speaks first. "Kermit the Frog's eye is popping out of your head."

I rub the spot that made contact with the table. It's the size of a Ping-Pong ball.

"Don't move," Mom says slowly, using her I-have-everything-under-control voice. "I'll get an ice pack."

Drew rushes off without asking to be excused. Mom gives me a Boo-Boo Buddy, an ice pack in the shape of a little pig we keep stashed in the freezer. I place the cold pig lightly on top of my bump. It's throbbing, but it only hurts when I press it.

"She doesn't have to go to the emergency room," Drew says, sitting back down, his video camera in hand. "I looked it up. She needs ice and Tylenol. The swelling will go down on its own. It's called a goose egg." He takes a bite of chicken like nothing happened, then points his camera at me. I roll my eyes up into my head and stick my tongue out.

"Abby knows all about goose eggs," Mom says, putting a Tylenol pill in front of me. I swallow it without water. "She whapped herself in the head all the time as a toddler."

"The mystery is solved," Drew says. I pinch him. "OW!" he yells.

"That's enough," Dad says, his jaw twitching. "Give me your phone, Abby."

"But I'm wounded! Please, Dad."

Dad's hand swoops across the table and snatches my phone. He slides it into his shirt pocket. "You'll get it back when you learn how to behave at the table. You got hurt because you were fooling around. You have to be more careful." Dad takes Drew's camera away too. Dinner is pretty much quiet after that.

Later, I'm up in my room reading *Entertainment Weekly* when there's a knock on my door. "I'm not playing Xbox," I say. Drew probably wants to play *Clash of Zombies.* The door opens. It's Mom and Dad. Why are they in my room? "Did my teacher call? I interrupted him in class today, but he didn't get mad, I swear."

"He did call," Dad says. I knew Tony was too good to be true. "But just to introduce himself. Is it true he lets you call him by his first name?" I nod, relieved I'm not in trouble. "Hmph. Well, *Tony* told us to email him anytime. I might do that."

"Please don't."

Mom sits next to me and lifts the Boo-Boo Buddy, peering at my forehead. "Much better."

"So that's why you guys are here?" I ask. "To let me know my teacher called to say hi?"

"That," Mom says, "and to say good job on keeping up with your English homework this week," Mom says. "We checked online."

So that's what this visit is about, to show me they're going to be "hands-on" from now on, emailing Tony and cyber-spying on me. I curse whoever invented the Internet. "Okay, well, if there isn't anything else, I'm just waiting for my concussion to set in, so . . ." I go back to my magazine.

Mom takes it out of my hands. "You don't have a concussion, poo poo poo." I'm not sure what this "poo poo poo" superstition is all about, but Jewish women say it constantly. Basically, it's a reminder not to get too excited about good luck, because some jealous witch out there could be saying, "I'll get you, my pretty," and drop a house on you. Unless, of course, you say "poo poo poo" to prevent this from happening.

"I want to remind you of the things Dr. C talked about," Mom says. "Are you going to remember to take your meds every day and tell us the truth?"

"And control your mouth?" Dad puts in.

"Sure, no problem." *Blah, blah, blah.*

"Good." Mom gets up and opens my closet, revealing my messy hill of clothes and shoes.

"I'll clean that up tomorrow," I say.

She pulls a Forever 21 shopping bag off a high shelf and hands it to me. How long has that been there?

"What's that?" Dad asks, as mystified as me.

I open it and pull out a pair of jeans in exactly the right shade of blue; an aqua tank with a red, sparkly star; and red sequined flip-flops. "Blue jeans, not too light, not too dark, like you said," Mom says. "The star is because you want to be a star. I can return everything if you don't like it."

"No, no, no, I love it all!" I hug her carefully with one arm, holding the clothes in the other one. Why is she doing this? "Thank you . . . but I thought you liked me better in skirts."

"I do. But you like jeans." She kisses the top of my head.

I can't get over it. After everything I've put my parents through, I'm getting presents. It doesn't add up. But since they're suddenly so happy with me, I ask Dad, "Can I get my phone back now?"

"Let's not get crazy," he says. He doesn't seem as happy about the outfit.

"How about tomorrow?" I ask him.

"We'll see," Mom answers for him. "It's nine o'clock."

"Oh, come on, it's the weekend," I say. "The best shows start now. I was just about to come downstairs!" But they turn off the lights as they leave, closing the door behind them. I'm not even in my pj's yet. This early bedtime is ridiculous. Being grounded is ridiculous.

I hear Dad as they go downstairs. "A gift? You should have discussed it with me first, especially after her behavior at dinner."

"It's motivation," Mom answers. "We had a heavy session at the doctor's. Abby needs an incentive. She won't make any progress without rewards."

I won't make any progress without rewards? Really?

This outfit is a dog biscuit. Mom thinks I can't get my act together by myself. She doesn't think I can get through summer school without messing up, or that I can be trusted again, or remember my meds, or get anything right unless she throws me a bone.

Woof.

I guess Tony did the same thing with the stand-up comedy reward. More dog-bone giving. They have the same doubts I do, that I can't change on my own.

My parents think they're always right about everything, and I don't want to encourage that, but—and it hurts to admit this—incentives will probably work for me. At the same time, what my parents and Tony don't understand is that, deep down, I'm starting to *want* to change, and not just to get a reward.

Then again, getting these new clothes doesn't stink. I try everything on. I'll be wearing this new outfit when I do my stand-up comedy, for sure.

17

Spoiler Alert.

"What would you say if I said you could read a novel in an hour?" Tony asks on Monday.

This week is off to a good start. The bump on my head went down a lot, and I got an A on a pop quiz. I took it at the empty table. Then I moved back to my regular seat. Nobody asked me any questions about it.

"What do you think, folks?" Tony asks.

I raise my hand as high as I can and flick my hand like it's on fire. My arm is about to come out of its socket. *Pickmepickmepickme.*

"Graham, what do you think?" Judging by Graham's disinterested face and Tony Hawk shirts, he doesn't have any opinions except on whether it's a good day to hit the skateboard park. "Nah. Not possible." He wasn't even raising his hand. Not fair.

Mine is still up. Tony turns around. I can't wait anymore. "You *can* read it in an hour!" My sentences spill out, rolling over each other. "If you're on an airplane going through a time zone, and you arrive at the same time you took off, *but* you had extra hours on the plane because of the time change, you could read it in an hour since you're in a new time zone, and you get to set your clock back."

Sofia and her friends start talking in Spanish, and I overhear Graham say to Kelvin, "She better get that bump on her head checked."

"Shut up, Graham!" I say.

"Settle down, both of you," Tony says. "And Abby, please raise your hand."

"But it was raised."

Trina leans toward me. "You're right. Time is an illusion." Figures Trina would get it.

Tony holds up a book with a girl in Shakespearean clothes on the cover. The title is *Mary of Stratford.* "You're going to read this book in an hour. First step, take out chapters one and two." He gets scissors from his desk, and cuts pages out of *Mary of Stratford.* "Chapter one, ladies and gents. He tosses the book to Trina. She catches it. "Remove chapter two, please, Trina."

She turns the book over in her hands. "I can't."

"What's the matter, haven't you ever had the urge to rip something to shreds?" he asks her.

"I have that urge every day," I blurt. "I rip everything from magazines to clothes." Tony shakes his head at me. I'm talking too much.

"Kelvin rips bean bombers," Graham says.

"You rip some back draft yourself, bro," Kelvin shoots back. They fist bump. Tony shushes them and tells them to come see him after class.

"Destroying a book is bad karma," Trina says. "Schools in Africa don't have books."

Max raises his hand. Tony calls on him. "What if every student brings in a book," Max says, "and then we donate it to a school or library that needs it?"

Trina decides this will even out the karma equation, so she carefully cuts out chapter two. I cut chapters three and four. Max gets five and six, and Amy has seven and eight. *Mary of Stratford* makes its way around the room, getting slashed, piece by piece. Tony tells us to keep what we rip, cut, or tear, and read it silently.

When we're finished, Tony has each person stand up and explain what they read. We go in order, so Tony is first, Trina is second, I'm third, Max is fourth, and so on. When it's Amy's turn, people go, "We can't hear you!" She stops and starts, stumbles over her

107

words. I guess she really doesn't like to talk—not just to us. It's painful. I feel bad for her.

After Amy, it goes quickly. As each person has a turn, we piece together the murder mystery. Once in a while someone goes, "*Now* I get it!"

In the middle of Sofia's turn, like a flash, the killer's identity comes to me. "IT'S ANNE! Mary's friend Anne did it!"

For a split second everything is still, like that moment of calm at the beach right before a wave knocks you down.

Then the class turns on me with jabs like "You ruined it!" and "What is WRONG with you?!" Kelvin sweeps everything off his table and onto the floor, scattering pages everywhere. "Thanks a lot, Spoiler Alert. That's your new name. Spoiler Alert."

"Sorry, sorry, sorry," I plead. "I just guessed."

"Kelvin, that is enough. Pick everything up, please. Abby, keep your guesses to yourself in the future."

But Kelvin isn't done. "Spoiler Alert," he keeps saying. A few more voices call out "Spoiler Alert, Spoiler Alert."

It feels like they're stomping on me. I lower my head and turn to the side so my hair is a curtain. I don't want them to see my face.

"I like knowing the ending early," Trina says to me. "Suspense is too stressful. It's good you spilled it. Now I can relax."

"Spoiler Alert," Kelvin says.

Sofia flashes her long fingernails at Kelvin. "Stop it, okay?" Her nails are manicured with a black-and-gold design. "We're almost done with this crazy story anyway." Her friends murmur in Spanish and nod, making their ponytails bob.

I'm about to ask Tony for the bathroom pass so I can escape, when Max, louder than I've ever heard him, goes, "*You're* the spoiler alert, Kelvin! Abby only guessed. You said she was right. So, really, *you're* the spoiler alert." Max to my rescue?

Kelvin doesn't have a chance to shoot back, because Tony's razor-sharp tone cuts him off. "Kelvin, see me after class."

Everyone is quiet after that. It turns out Anne was the murderer. I was right.

When we're done with the book-cutting activity, Tony says, "You guys read that book in an hour. Good job!" He flings loose pages up with both hands. They rain down like confetti. "Let's celebrate!"

Kelvin's quad follows Tony's lead. Graham picks up pages off the floor and throws them around. Sofia's group goes completely bananas, hurling chapters everywhere. I halfheartedly crumple a few pages and toss them at Max. Normally, this is my kind of scene, but I'm still recovering from the "spoiler alert" attack. Trina and Amy sit back and watch everyone going crazy.

"WHAT is happening in here?" demands a shrill, high voice. It's Mrs. Shoop, the vice principal, standing in our doorway. The chattering and page tossing dies down. Mrs. Shoop is thin and nervous and always adjusting the cardigans she keeps tied around her shoulders.

Tony rubs his hands together. "Good morning, Mrs. Shoop." Her eyebrows knit together as she scans the room. Bits and pieces of *Mary of Stratford* are scattered across the floor and tables. "You'll explain this, er, unorthodox process to me later, Mr. Norton, m'kay?"

"Glad to, Mrs. Shoop," Tony says.

She points at the mess on the floor. "I expect you all to take care of this, m'kay?"

Tony chuckles after she closes the door. "Guess it's time to clean up, guys."

"M'kay?" I add. I get a few "m'kays" back, plus some laughs.

❋

Before we leave for break, Tony calls me up to his desk. "Are you all right, Abby? The kids were tough on you." I nod, glad he's not mad at me for giving away the ending. "I was going to tell you this Friday would be a good day for you to do your stand-up comedy performance, but I think we need to put it on hold. I'm sorry."

"Why?"

"We made a deal that you weren't going to call out or interrupt, remember?" My face falls. "Did you take your medicine?" he asks.

"Yes. I've been really good about remembering."

"Hmm. You usually do well in the mornings. Why do you think you had a hard time controlling yourself today?"

I think about that. "Class was different than usual. We weren't sitting doing something boring like workbook . . . we were cutting paper and throwing it, and it all felt like a mystery game, you know, with figuring out the book."

"So you forgot about our deal? Maybe got a little too involved with the game part of it?"

"I guess so, yeah."

"Well, if you can keep up your end of our deal all week, then I'll pick another Friday, and we'll be back on, okay? Look at me." I didn't realize I wasn't. I lift my head. "What if, when you're beginning to spin out of control, I touch my chin twice, like this?" He taps his chin twice. "That'll be our secret signal between us, so I don't have to tell you in front of the class not to shout or raise your hand." He taps his chin twice again. "Okay?"

I tap my chin twice and nod.

18

This could be a disaster.

The four of us are sitting at our picnic table outside during snack time. It's been a week and a half, so by now I know what everybody eats. Amy, Max, and I buy bagels, packets of strawberry jam, and milk from the cafeteria. Trina brings fancy organic seaweed crackers from home.

Amy and I spread jam on our bagels while Trina pulls out a sketch pad and pencil case painted with mythical creatures. "Did you paint that?" I ask, amazed by her talent.

"Yeah. I paint walls, doors, furniture. My parents

are artists, so they let me." She pulls out markers and starts drawing.

Max taps his laptop's touch pad furiously. He makes a growling noise, taps some more. "Uch, it's frozen. I hate when it does this."

Trina holds out her hands. "I've got this."

Max gives her the laptop but says, "Don't bother. I broke it when I dropped it."

Trina clicks on some icons, types, taps, then hands it back to him.

He is beyond awestruck. "How did you do that? You fixed it! It never unfreezes that fast. It takes hours."

Trina's already switched off and gone back to her dragon drawing. When Caitlin said Trina invented an app, I didn't believe it, but how did she fix Max's computer problem in two seconds? I've never seen her on a computer. Techies are usually glued to some device. It doesn't make sense.

"Did you know the dragon myth was inspired by dinosaurs and crocodiles?" Max asks us.

I'm curious about Trina. "Trina, did you—"

"Watch this," Max says, talking over me. He takes out playing cards from his backpack, flips an ace of spades playing card, then flicks it, turning it into the queen of hearts. Amy claps.

"Trina—"

Max waves his hand in my face. Now it's the ace

of spades again. "The dragon myth was an illusion. What ancient people thought they saw wasn't there."

"Stop interrupting me, Max! Trina, is it true—"

"Uh-oh," Amy says, pointing at my new jeans. She never interrupts. I look down to where she's pointing. It's a big red blob on my thigh. Strawberry jam.

My new jeans from Mom. Stained. Ruined. A feeling of dread comes over me. "I've got to get this out." I rub it with my napkin, but it spreads instead. Now it's bigger.

"Uh-oh," Amy says again. I bet she never spills.

"That's not going to come out," Max says. "I know. I do the laundry at home."

"For your whole family?" Trina asks, tuning back in. Her eyes are foggy, like we woke her up.

I'm about to ask Max why he does the laundry when Trina shocks me by leaning over and drawing on my jeans with a thick black marker.

"Hey!" I shout, pushing her hand away.

She smiles. "Just breathe, Abby. This isn't a laptop, but I can fix it too. Watch."

Amy and Max give me freak-out face.

Trina, on the other hand, is as calm as a Hindu cow. "I hope you like dragons." She draws on my thigh again, all around the stain. "Don't. Move."

This could be a disaster.

19

I am a jerk.

Mom must have gone blind, because she hasn't noticed my jeans until now. We're in Publix with Drew buying canned goods for his Feed the Hungry bar mitzvah charity project. I didn't have time to change.

"What . . . is . . . that?" she asks, pointing at my thigh. Apparently, her vision is not impaired.

"A dragon!" I answer, excited. "Don't worry. Trina used permanent markers, so the colors won't run. She's an artist." Mom blinks in confusion. "See, I spilled strawberry jam on them, so she turned the red spot into fire from the dragon's mouth."

"Let me understand this. You had someone *draw* all over them after I *just* bought them."

"I like it," Drew puts in.

"No one will have a pair like these," I say proudly.

"They certainly won't." Her lips disappear. I hold my breath. Then she goes, "I can't deal with this today. Get canned goods, both of you. Meet me at checkout in ten minutes. And, Abby? Stop with the strawberry jam. I mean it."

"But it's fruit!"

"It's sugar and red food coloring!" She wheels the cart away like she's on a mission to run someone over with it.

"Mom was on the phone with Aunt Roz this afternoon," Drew tells me. "You know that always makes her grumpy." He crouches down to get a closer look at the dragon. "It's awesome. Mom doesn't get it."

"Mom doesn't get *me*," I answer.

He stands up. "Yeah, well, Dad doesn't get *me*."

Drew and I snag a cart to share and horse around in the canned-vegetables aisle. Mom rolls up to us. "What do you two think you're doing? Why are you only filling your cart with beans?" Drew and I look at each other. We don't exactly know why. A shopping cart full of beans seemed hilarious a minute ago.

"They're good for your heart?" is my answer. Drew chimes in with fart noises. Mom rolls her cart away.

The two of us wander around some more, then split up. Mom always allows Drew and me two items each. I get a celebrity magazine and a vanilla sachet from the candle section. Maybe if I smell like vanilla the way Amy does, I'll be perfect like her too. Drew gets M&M's and a Stephen King book about a woman who chops up her husband with an axe. In the checkout line, I lift my sachet to my nose to smell it, but it falls out of my hand.

Someone behind me bends down to pick it up before I do, and we almost bump heads. It's Max!

We both say hi. He hands me the sachet. He's with his dad. Our parents introduce themselves. Max's dad has icky groceries—zucchini bread and a jar of something called Lemonaise.

Not that our groceries are normal. "Wow, your family eats a lot of beans," says Max.

"It's for a donation," Mom answers quickly.

"Yes, we're donating gas," I say.

Max lets out a laugh without thinking. I've never seen him smile. His braces are blue like mine. Maybe Magic Max has a sense of humor after all.

"Abby!" Mom says, embarrassed. I'm the one who should be embarrassed. Mom is wearing a KATY PERRY OR DIE T-shirt.

"You know what's interesting?" Max says, his eyes flicking to me, then back to my mom as he scans our cans. "People don't usually buy vegetables or

117

legumes at night. They buy them in the morning. At night, you see a lot of meat."

"That *is* interesting," Drew says, because he loves strange and useless information like that.

The pimply high school boy behind the cash register stops scanning bean cans to put the sachet up to his nose. He takes a deep whiff. "Would you like a separate bag for this?" He tries to hand it to Mom, who doesn't take it.

Mom folds her arms. "Why would I want my daughter to use that sachet after you've rubbed your nose on it?"

Drew and I look for the closest exit. Mom may only be five foot two, but when she sinks her teeth into something—or someone—this woman is a category five hurricane, an eighteen-wheeler driving at full speed, a sledgehammer. She won't be ignored.

"Why would I buy it now that you've soiled it?" Mom asks the cashier.

Drew wanders out of the line, pretending he doesn't know us. I start to follow, but Mom stands in my way. Who says "soiled" to a person? I am *dying* that Max is witnessing this.

The cashier stammers, "Ma'am, I—I didn't rub my nose on it, I j-just sme—"

"Excuse me?" Mom interrupts. She hates being called ma'am. In her delusional midlife-crisis mind, this boy might as well have said, "Hi there, old lady."

"May I speak to the manager, please?"

This is SO embarrassing. "Mom," I say through clenched teeth. "You do *not* need to speak to the manager." I turn to the cashier, who I feel really sorry for because when Mom is done with him, his skin will break out even more, probably. "I don't want the sachet anymore. Sorry." He looks at my mother, terrified.

Mom takes out her wallet. "Fine, take it off the bill." She pays.

Drew and I load the cart with bags, I wave at Max, and we hurry toward the exit. Hallelujah.

"Abby, wait!" I turn around as Max walks up to me. "Can I talk to you for a second?"

"Sure," I say with a quick glance at Mom. "But I have to go."

Mom stops her cart. "No, that's okay. You two talk. We'll wait for you in the car, Abby." Talk about a mood swing. I guess she's happy I might have another friend besides Caitlin. She's never been a fan of Caitlin, for some reason.

Max's words come out of his mouth fast, as if he rehearsed them. "Well, uh, you're really funny, and I know you're into drama and you're comfortable performing in front of people and everything, so I was wondering . . . if you might want to work with me."

"Huh?"

He clears his throat. "Like, help me with my job as a magician."

"You mean you get paid to do magic?"

"Not in money. I get community-service hours. I know you need them, and I thought because you're funny and everything, maybe we could work as a team. You know, like Penn and Teller, those magicians in Las Vegas?"

"No, I don't know them."

"Well, Penn has all the personality, and Teller doesn't talk."

"So you want me to be Penn and you to be Teller?"

"Something like that, yeah."

"But no money, right? I owe my dad a lot of money."

"You would get paid in other ways."

"What would I get paid in, balloon animals? Connected handkerchiefs?"

"Uh, no. You would get paid in experience and . . . community-service hours . . ." His voice trails off. I wait for him to say something else. He doesn't. He tries another grin. There's something sweet about the way he does it.

For a split second, the idea seems almost good. I picture myself in a leotard with a cute skater skirt, picking volunteers from the audience, pulling them up onstage, joking with them. "Where are these magic shows?" I ask.

"The youth community center or old age homes.

Hospitals. I have one coming up at Chuck E. Cheese's. Oh, and I did the Garlic Festival in Delray."

He's got to be kidding. Little kids, the elderly, and housewives. "Wow, Max, will the excitement never cease? I don't know if there's room for me in your life of glitz and glamour."

He looks as if I've slapped him.

I instantly feel awful. My mouth strikes again. "Sorry," I say. "I didn't think. I—"

"No, it's okay. It was a stupid idea."

"It's not a stupid idea. Not at all. You're a good magician. I'll think about it. Okay?" He doesn't answer, just clomps away in his big sneakers. I am a mean, horrible person. "Max . . . I didn't mean to . . ." But he's at the door, going back to his dad. "Your magic shows sound great, really!" The hurt in his eyes is hard to take.

Because I caused it. Why do I say these things? WHY?

Dr. C's voice is in my mind: *You have to slow down in social situations. Stop and think about how a person will feel before you say out loud whatever pops into your head.*

Now Max hates me. And he's so nice.

I am a jerk.

When I get in the car, Mom says, "Is everything okay?"

"Yeah." I lean my forehead against the window. "He

had a question about homework, that's all." She'll just make me feel worse and tell me to Think Before I Speak. *Yes, Mom, my mouth is still a verbal wrecking ball.* I know Drew can tell I'm lying, but he doesn't push for info. He tries to cheer me up by showing me a video on his phone of our school nurse whipping her hair back and forth at the spring dance. It doesn't help.

I can't get through one day without screwing up or hurting someone's feelings.

Who am I kidding about being able to change?

20

You're a star, not a meteor.

Max is quiet at school today. He barely talks to any of us and won't look at me.

At break, when he leaves to get a drink from the vending machine, I tell Trina and Amy what happened at Publix. "You should perform with him," Trina says. She *would* say that. Trina's hardware is missing the embarrassment chip. Today she's wearing Hello Kitty pajama pants, a baseball T-shirt, and holey socks with sandals. "You two would rock a magic show."

"Yeah," Amy agrees, sipping her fruit punch.

"But I don't *want* to rock a magic show in subarfia," I say. "Poco Bay, Florida, the land of shopping centers and golf, is not my destiny." I bite into my plain bagel, no strawberry jam.

"It is, for now," Trina says. "So open yourself up to the idea."

"I wish I was in Hollywood already," I complain. "Or at least Camp Star Lake."

Trina waves her seaweed cracker at me. "If you really want to be a star, then maybe it's a *good* thing you didn't go to that drama camp. If you had, maybe you'd only be a meteor, not a star."

"What do you mean?" I ask her.

"Think about it. Meteors shoot out in a flash, light up the sky, and then"—she snaps her fingers—"disappear. If you'd gone to camp, a talent agent would have come to see the shows, you'd have been discovered, gone on TV or in movies, you'd be an overnight sensation, right?"

"Right!" I answer, picturing it, loving it. "What's wrong with that?"

"Overnight sensations disappear." Trina takes a bite of her seaweed cracker, chews, and swallows. "Stars, on the other hand, glow for billions of years. It takes a little longer for their light to be seen, but once they show up, they're around pretty much forever. So it's worth the wait. Maybe the universe has bigger things planned for you than being a meteor, you know what I'm saying?"

I do know what she's saying.

Amy, of all people, confirms it by saying it—whispering it, really—out loud. "You're a star, not a meteor." She pats my arm awkwardly.

I don't know if it's Trina's philosophy or Amy's gesture, but they almost make me cry.

Back in class, I try a do-over with Max. "What kinds of tricks do you do for your magic shows, Max?"

"That's okay," he says. "You don't have to pretend you're interested. I can tell when you're lying."

"Eyes on me, people," Tony says, clapping to get the class's attention. "What are the themes in *A Midsummer Night's Dream*?"

I raise my hand. If I'm right, Max will love it. "I've got one! What about—"

Tony taps his chin twice.

The signal. I stop talking, keep my hand still and wait. Tony calls on me. "Magic," I announce.

"Good. Very important theme," Tony says, writing *magic*. Amy copies it into her notebook. Yes! I *did* understand it. I check Max for a reaction. He doesn't look up. "Many characters are under the influence of magic."

Later, Tony wants to know if anyone would like to read their creative-writing assignment. I volunteer first. "Anyone else?" Tony asks, scanning the room. My hand is the only one up. "No one else? No? Anyone? Okay. Abby."

"Our topic was art forms," I tell everyone. "My art form is acting. I wrote a poem."

I put on my best dramatic voice.

"Wherefore must I be stuck in school, which
    stinketh so?
Will not I ever star in my own TV show?
Will I get to pursue my passion—
Acting, which I plan to make cash in?
Wast I adopted, or am I truly related to my
    insane family?
Yea, these questions, much like the wee black
    thingies in a slice of salami,
Are a mystery."

The only one who doesn't clap and laugh is Max. I should feel warm and fuzzy. Everyone else got a kick out of my poem, and I got the Shakespeare question right. But Max is taking the shine off everything.

I wish he would look at me.

21

No, what's crazy is that you lost a whole human being and a wheelchair.

This is *not* how I want to spend my Saturday, but my community service starts today, so here I am. For a place that's supposed to cheer up the elderly, Millennium Lakes is not exactly uplifting. It has silk plants, plastic flowers, and a pukey smell of vinyl, rubbing alcohol, and corn.

In the hallway an ancient woman in a nightgown shuffles up to me and goes, "*Psssst.* Be careful. They're all loan sharks here." What are loan sharks? It sounds like something Grandpa would know. I'll ask him later.

Mom and Dad already filled out my registration

online, so Bonnie, the activities director, only has to give me a tour and a brief training session before she wheels out an old-timer with bushy, wilderness-man eyebrows. She orders me to keep an eye on him (hello, it's not like he can run away) and sprints off in her squeaky shoes so "you two can get acquainted."

"Hi," I say to Crazy Brows. "Um . . . so . . . how are you today?"

He wheels himself away from me. "How do you think I am? I'm eighty-six, my wife and friends are dead, and my kids don't visit their father, who could die at any moment."

I grab hold of the back handles, stopping him. "Well, you don't look a day over eighty-five." He looks so small in the wheelchair with his little feet in thick socks and rubber-soled shoes. "I'm Abby."

He grunts. "Abby, you look like you're starving to death. I hope you're not one of those girls who throw up all the time. My name is Simon Eppelmeyer." Why couldn't I get a sweet grandpa in a fuzzy sweater and bifocals, like in Thanksgiving commercials?

Except for barking "Slow down!" Simon doesn't say anything while I steer him along the footpaths outside. I tell him how I was in a wheelchair too when I was eight, after I got the idea to rollerblade in an empty pool. I broke a bone in one leg and tore a ligament in the other. "You make me feel real safe" is all he says after I finish my story.

The fresh air is a relief after the yucky smell inside. Hibiscus bushes, benches, a duck pond. Simon's eyes are closed. He's asleep. I roll the wheelchair under a banyan tree with a humongous trunk full of twisted roots. Then I sit on the bench next to it and pull out the half-eaten power bar in my pocket. I wonder if ducks like power bars. I walk down a slope to the pond's edge, break off pieces, and try to feed them. Turns out they don't. More for me, I guess. I finish it, throw a few pebbles in the water, and check the time on my phone. It's been a half hour. Time to return Simon.

When I get back to the bench, my stomach drops like a broken elevator.

The wheelchair isn't there. Simon is gone.

GONE.

"Simon!" I call. No answer. "SIMON!" I run down the path, around and around the edge of the pond until my sneakers are muddy. I don't see him.

What do I do?

Wait. Up ahead on the footpath. That might be him. In that wheelchair a nurse is pushing. *Pleasebe SimonpleasebeSimonpleasebeSimon.*

It's not Simon.

The nurse disappears down the path. How did I lose a person *in a wheelchair?*

I am so *stupid.* A loser. Of old people. On my first day! All Bonnie asked me to do was keep an eye on

129

him, and I couldn't even do that. "SIMON!" I scream in desperation, looking out across the pond.

What if he drowned? What if he followed me down to the pond, lost control of the wheelchair, and—

No. Impossible. I would have heard a splash or something.

Right?

I rush toward the building. I have to tell Bonnie. I need help. Then I see him.

Not Simon. Standing in the middle of the path is Max. A feeling comes over me, a kind of peace, and a sense that everything is going to be okay. Max will come to my rescue. He'll find Simon for me.

I approach him and Bonnie. "Hey, Max! Are you doing a magic show here?"

"You two know each other?" Bonnie asks. I nod. "Small world. Max will indeed be doing a magic show for our residents. Where is Simon?"

Oh, God. "Um . . . I . . ." *Tell her you lost him!* "I . . . left Simon with another volunteer . . . nurse lady. She's watching him for a minute." And with that statement, I plaster on a fat fake smile to match the fat, fake whopper I just told. *Now you've done it, Abby. You'd better find him. Fast.*

Max is giving me a strange look. And then I remember what he said yesterday: *I can tell when you're lying.*

Bonnie's phone chimes. She reads a text. "Gotta

130

take care of this. Max, I'll finish showing you around next time." Then she turns to me. "Bring Simon inside for lunch in fifteen minutes."

She's off, leaving me face-to-face with Max. "Listen, I know you hate me after what I said at Publix about your magic shows, which, by the way, I totally take back. I think you doing magic shows for community service is awesome and—"

"I don't hate you," he interrupts. "But I have to go." He starts to leave.

"Max, wait, I *need* you."

He stops. "Huh?"

"I know sometimes I say and do things I shouldn't before my brain pulls the brakes. I'm working on it. I go to a doctor and everything. But listen—"

"You go to a doctor in this place?"

"Why would I go to a doctor here?! What am I, ninety?" I hunch over, suck my lips over my teeth like I'm toothless. "Hello, sonny . . ."

Max's lips form a hint of a smile. "I have no clue what's going on with you, but I have stuff to do for, what was it you said? My life of glitz and glamour. Yeah, that was it." He starts to leave again.

"Max, please!" I go after him. "Don't be like this." I stop, suddenly tired of this back-and-forth game with him. I grab the back of his shirt.

"Whoa, personal space," he says, turning around.

I let go. "Haven't you ever given someone another

chance even if they've done something to hurt you? Caitlin hurts my feelings all the time, but I don't throw her away."

That gets to him. He looks like he's thinking hard.

I need to tell him about Simon already. "Here's the sitch. I lost a man out here."

"What do you mean you lost a man? Like, *killed* him?"

"Shhhh!" My eyes dart around to make sure the coast is clear. "No, I took him for a walk. One minute he was sleeping in his wheelchair, and the next minute he disappeared."

Max grins. Then laughs. "I'll have to find out how he does that. Maybe I could use it in my act."

For once I'm not happy someone is laughing at my shenanigans. "Max, stop." But he's laughing his head off. "I have this feeling you can help me find Simon. It sounds crazy, I know."

"No, what's crazy is that you lost a whole human being *and* a wheelchair." He cracks up all over again. "I'll help you find him on one condition." He looks down at me, the sun hitting him like a spotlight. His eyes are the lightest brown eyes I've ever seen, the color of baby Bambi, or a gym floor.

"Anything."

"Do a magic show with me."

I have a vision of myself standing in an aisle at Costco, holding a rabbit, surrounded by moms chomping on food samples. Max is there too, waving a magic wand at crying brats in shopping carts. He and I look like the world's biggest doofuses.

I can't do it.

Max reads my face, shakes his head.

Simon.

"Okay!" I shout. "I'll do it!"

We retrace the brick-lined path down to the duck pond, even checking the bushes. Where *is* he? *Please let Simon be okay.*

I plop down on the bench, feeling my heart sink with failure and fear. What if something terrible happened to Simon because of me? Max is somewhere behind me, walking on a patch of grass around the big banyan tree. I stand back up and brace myself to go tell Bonnie.

"Wait a sec," Max says. "Did you know that the most important part of being an illusionist is distracting the audience so they don't notice what trick you're really pulling?" Max's eyes are fixed on the tree.

"Thanks, David Blaine, but what does that have to do with—" He reaches up near my ear and plucks a small twig from the space where my shoulder meets my neck. "A good illusionist makes you think he's doing one thing while he's really doing something else, and before you know it . . ." This time his fingers lightly brush my ear. A tingly feeling travels down my neck. He brings his hand back, opens it up, and shows me a pink hibiscus flower in the center of his palm.

I snatch the flower from him and flick his forehead with it. Simon could be rolling down the highway by now, and Max is wasting my time with magic? "Nice trick, but I have to report Simon missing. Thanks for your help." I guess my idea that Max would find Simon was wishful thinking. I start up the path.

"I wouldn't do that if I were you," Max says.

"Well, you're not me. You didn't lose a person, okay?"

"I know where he is," Max says.

I turn around. Max juts his chin toward the tree. Then I follow him as he leads me around the trunk to the other side, where there's an enormous teardrop-shaped opening in it the size of a door.

Max points for me to walk through it, so I do. I'm inside the hollow trunk. It would almost feel like a

dark closet if it weren't for the ray of sunlight stream-
ing through, shining on Simon, fully awake and sitting comfortably in the wheelchair.

Simon!

"He wasn't sleeping," Max explains.

Simon has been here the whole time! *In a tree.* I
want to fall to my knees and bawl like a baby, I'm so
relieved. Simon points at me with his long, ET-ish
finger. "Gotcha! You kept passing by me, over and
over."

Another flood of relief rushes through me.

Quickly followed by anger. Because as much as
I want to hug Simon for being okay, I also want to
rip his furry eyebrows off. "Why did you do that?!" I
shout. "Here I was, thinking you might be dead, and
it was a *prank*? How was I supposed to find you IN
A TREE?"

"What? This is a tree?" he asks, serious all of a
sudden. "I'm not in a tree." His eyes roam up, down,
disoriented. "Where am I? What are you talking
about?"

Think and *respond.* Don't *react.* Maybe Simon is a
few sandwiches short of a picnic, only I didn't realize
it before. "Where do you think you are?" I ask him
carefully.

He scratches his head. "Uh . . . in a nutshell . . ."

"Yes?"

His eyes twinkle. "That's it. I'm in a nutshell." He laughs. Well, wheezes, really. "Gotcha! Again!"

"Not funny," I say. It figures that out of all the patients here, I get assigned the one-man show. I'll probably be like him when I'm old. Why don't his children visit him? What if one day he's really gone for good, and he never got to see his kids? I'm going to ask Bonnie if she'll let me get in touch with them and ask them to visit.

"*I* thought it was funny," Max says as I wheel Simon out of the tree trunk.

"Oh, so now suddenly you can take a joke?" I ask him.

"Sure, when it's not on me." He grabs the handles of the wheelchair and pushes Simon for me. We start making our way up the path.

Simon looks at Max. "Who are you?"

"I'm Max," he answers with a wave.

"You can call him Magic Max," I say to Simon. I guess my feeling was right after all, about Max being here to help me out. "I owe you one," I say to Max. I give him a quick hug.

I'll have to do a magic show with him now. I don't want to, but what choice do I have?

After what he did for me today, it's only fair.

23

Don't pretend you didn't like Hannah Montana, once upon a time.

Tony lifts a tote bag from behind his desk and hands it to me. "Abby, please collect the book donations. Thank you."

Max drops *The Secret Life of Houdini* in the tote. "Did you read those magic articles I gave you?" he asks.

"I lost them," I admit. "Can you give them to me again?"

"Sure. You can read them online. I'll get you the links." He's so eager for me to be his assistant. It racks me with guilt. I Googled Penn and Teller. How can Max like them? They are lunatics. Magic isn't my thing. I *have* to get out of this, but I don't know how.

Max's light brown eyes are peering at me, all hopeful and puppy-like. "Yeah, send me the links," I say. I open my backpack and take out the book I'm donating, *Miles to Go* by Miley Cyrus.

Max palms his forehead. "Miley Cyrus? You actually *read* that?" His blue braces make a rare appearance in a two-foot-wide grin. "That's hilarious."

"I was curious," I say sheepishly. "Don't pretend you didn't like Hannah Montana, once upon a time."

"Never," Max says.

"I did," Amy whispers.

"I never watched *Hannah Montana,*" Trina says. "I mean, I know who she is from seeing her on lunch boxes and T-shirts, but I wasn't allowed to have a TV until this year."

"I'm still not allowed to have a TV in my room," Max says.

"Me either," Amy and I say together.

"No . . ." Trina rolls her hair into a bun, then sticks two pencils in it. "I didn't have a TV *at all.* Like, I never watched TV until this year."

"WHAAAAT?" comes out of my mouth.

The pencils in the back of Trina's head look like antennae. "My parents have a TV in their bedroom for emergencies, but they don't watch it. I was allowed to start watching when I started seventh grade, but to be honest, I still don't watch."

Max, Amy, and I give each other knowing glances. That explains a lot about Trina.

I go around the room collecting books. Trina hands in one about an artist lady from Mexico with braids on her head and a mustache. Amy has one about Kate Middleton and the British royals. Sofia and her friends offer books in Spanish, while Kelvin's quad gives *Harry Potter* or picture books. Every single student remembered to bring in a donation. Pretty cool.

"I like celebrity biographies the best," I say, reading the back cover of the Kate Middleton book before handing over the bag to Tony.

"Me too," Amy says. At least, I'm pretty sure that's what I read her lips say.

"I like the ones about actresses," I tell her, dropping the Kate book back in the bag. "That's why I got the Miley Cyrus book. She was once a funny actress with a show, so I figured, why not check it out?"

I wait, but Amy doesn't say anything else.

"I like celeb magazines too, like *Entertainment Weekly*," I add.

"*Teen Vogue*," she says.

"I get those sometimes."

"And *Us Weekly*."

"My mother loves that one," I tell her.

"Mine too." She smiles. And then says nothing.

"Was that an actual conversation with Amy?" Max whispers in my ear.

"I think so," I whisper back.

Who knew I could have something in common with Amy? We both like celebrity books and magazines.

What would Caitlin say?

❋

It's eleven-thirty p.m. I've been in bed for over two hours, tossing and turning, wide awake. I might as well be a parked car with the engine left on, revved up and trapped.

I get up, stand in front of my mirror, and practice my red-carpet pose, smiling for the cameras in my imaginary glitzy dress. *You're a star, not a meteor.* Are Trina and Amy right?

Someday it's going to happen for me. It has to. My insides ache when I imagine my future on the stage, the big screen, the small screen, the everywhere-and-everything-in-between screen.

I scrounge in my closet and find hats from my Halloween collection. Perfect for characters. I do them in the mirror: police officer making an arrest, international assassin targeting her hit, blind skier reaching the summit. I sit at my desk, interviewing Tina Fey in my mind.

I'm in the mood to talk to a real person. I wish I had a friend to call.

Trina?

No. Trina may live in her own world, but I'm sure she knows, like I do, that this is a temporary summer school acquaintance situation. It's not a let's-text-each-other-and-be-best-buds scenario. I don't even have her number. It's not that kind of friendship.

But could it be?

Because, really, what do I have to lose if I text or call Trina? Or Max? Or Amy, even, although that would be a short conversation. Still. One of them might be awake like me, wondering if they should call.

I look up Trina's number in the summer school directory, enter it into my phone, and then plug in Max's and Amy's numbers too.

I stare at my phone. Then put it down.

The only person I'm comfortable calling is Caitlin, who is probably too busy pulling a prank with all her new, talented friends to talk to me.

I text her.

Me: How did ur monologue go? Did u get cast in the show?

Two seconds later, my phone dings. She's up.

Caitlin: Brett made it.

Me: You and Brett made it?

Caitlin: Just Brett

Me: Sorry

Caitlin: Auditioning 4 Legally Blonde. How's scrison (school+prison)?

Me: Hangin w/Max, Amy & Trina.

Caitlin: LOL! OK geek. Amy talks?

Me: Whispers. Laughs. Silently, natch.

I feel lousy writing that because Amy and I sort of connected today.

Caitlin: LOL Amy is a lump.

I don't answer her. Can't Caitlin say anything nice?

Caitlin: They r all losers.

I'm not telling her about Max and our upcoming magic show.

Me: What happened w/ur Kool-Aid prank?

Caitlin: The 2 who did it got kicked out

Me: But I thought u did it 2

Caitlin: Just watched

So Caitlin egged them on, then slithered out of it. Sounds familiar. Texting Caitlin was a mistake. She's even more venomous at camp than at home. Or am I just finally seeing the real her?

Caitlin: How's home life?

Me: Parentals go 2 CHADD meetings now. They r all up in my biz these days but I'm not as grounded as b4. Can do HW in room w/laptop

Caitlin: CHADD?

Me: Support group 4 parents of kids w/ADHD. They r all Ur phone is a privilege not a right. They keep taking phone away

Caitlin: Total child abuse. U NEED ur phone! GTG. We're sneaking out 2 boys cabin.

I wonder if Brett is up.

Hey Brett, how r u? Congratz on talent showcase! Text when u get a chance. ☺ Abby

No answer. I look at my clock. It's midnight. Time for bed.

24

Has Tony gone beyond the cliffs of insanity?

Has Tony gone beyond the cliffs of insanity? He just picked Amy to read the part of Hermia. Hasn't he noticed she can barely say her name at roll call? Amy looks like she wants to crawl under our table. She freezes, pencil in hand, her blue eyes terrified. I raise my hand and open my mouth to protest. It's cruel to put her through this.

Tony taps his chin twice. "Amy hasn't read a part yet," Tony says, looking straight at me, as if he's reading my mind.

I lower my hand. Tony acknowledges me with a tilt of his head.

"Go ahead, Amy," Tony says soothingly. "Stand up, and remember to speak loudly. You'll be fine." Trina gives her a thumbs-up, so Max and I do too.

Amy stands and opens her book. Her hands tremble. "'Be it so, Lysander: find you out a bed, for I upon this bank will rest my head. For my sake, my dear, lie further off yet, do not lie so near.'" Max, Trina, and I swap shocked, relieved expressions. Amy got through it fine, like Tony said she would.

So why is Amy so scared to open her mouth? Maybe it's only when she's using her own words that she clams up. When Amy sits back down, the three of us whisper "Good job" and "You did great" to her and stuff like that.

After class Tony calls me up to his desk. "You've showed good self-control lately, Abby. So . . . we're back on for your stand-up comedy performance. How does this Friday sound?"

A surge of happiness swells up in me. Now I'll get to show who I really am.

✳

Wednesday afternoons are the worst because it's not Friday yet, and comprehension questions are due every Thursday. I wish homework was something I could zip through, like Drew does. At least Mom let me go back to doing homework in my room with my laptop, but she won't give me the Wi-Fi password, so no Internet. Our class started this book called *King of Shadows,* which is a nice change from the play, but it's more work. Comprehension questions are so dumb.

Plus, I need to write jokes for my comedy routine Friday, except I can't think of any. On top of it all, we have our first big test next week. I don't know what to work on first.

I'm stuck. I pick up my pencil, smack it against my forehead, and break it in half. I can hear Drew and Dad outside, which doesn't help.

"OUCH!" Drew yells. I get off my bed and spy out the window. He's in the fetal position in the grass, the football next to him. Dad is standing over him.

"I'm having an asthma attack," Drew huffs. "I need my inhaler." Drew is close to tears. My heart aches for him.

Dad helps him up, gives him a comforting pat, and catches sight of me at the window. I fall back on my bed. It should be me out there, not my brother. But I'm not allowed to go outside until I'm finished with my homework.

I decide to take my chances. I go out to the back yard.

"Are you done?" Dad asks. I shake my head. "You can come back out when you've done all your work."

"Just ten minutes," I plead. "I have to get my wiggles out. Come on, Dad."

He stops, tosses the ball up, and catches it. "At CHADD, they said short, timed breaks are good for you to push the reset button before you get back to work," Dad says. "So. Ten minutes *only*." Drew goes inside.

Ten minutes turn into twenty, then thirty. We end up playing for an hour. I chase Dad into the bushes, getting my two-hand touch in just as he falls.

"Out of bounds," Dad says, grinning.

"No way, that was in! I got you!" I shout, catching my breath. I love the feel of my beating heart, the burn in my legs, my sweat-soaked skin. Free at last. "Howard," Mom calls from the patio. "She still has homework. It's time to come in."

"One more play," I say.

Mom shakes her head.

"Come on, Mom. Most parents *want* their kids outside. Do you know how lucky you are? Just one more play. Just one. Justonejustonejustonejustone."

Dad says, "Just one, Rachel. It's okay."

Mom throws up her hands and marches into the house.

I want my last kick to be earth-shatteringly awesome. Dad backs up all the way to the end of our yard. I run a few steps, pull my leg back, and kick the ball with all my strength, as if my life depends on it.

But something happens. Just as my toes make contact with the ball, my foot turns at a strange angle. The ball flies way away from Dad, high over his head, toward the house.

CRASH.

Dad and I stand frozen, looking at my bedroom window.

Or what used to be my bedroom window. My kick wasn't earth shattering. It was window shattering.

Mom is outside again. "What was that?!"

"Watch out for the glass!" Dad shouts. "It's everywhere."

"What happened?!" Mom shouts.

"Iaccidentallykickeditthroughthewindow," I babble. "I'm sorry. I didn't mean to. I'm sorry. I'm sorry."

That refreshing feeling of freedom I had earlier? Good-bye.

Mom points at Dad. "This is your fault. She should have come back in the house when I said so!"

"I was letting her take a break," Dad says.

Mom folds her arms. "Yeah, it was a break, all right. A break *in the window.* At the CHADD meeting, they said to be consistent, Howard." She walks away, mumbling.

"It's not Dad's fault!" I call after her. "It's mine!" I look at Dad. "Are you going to make me pay for the window?"

149

Dad hands me the football and puts his arm around me. "No. It was an accident. Nobody's fault. That's why they're called accidents." Then he lets out a long, twenty-pound sigh.

Everything is always my fault.

25

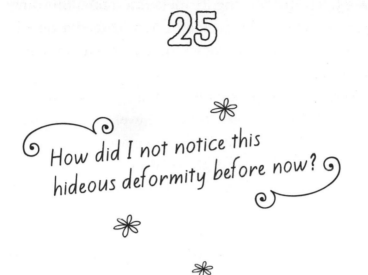

How did I not notice this hideous deformity before now?

Tony wanders the room, explaining our assignment. "Now that we've compared and contrasted examples of irony in *King of Shadows* and the play, I'd like you to write eight examples of irony from your own lives. Any questions? No? Good." Tony walks over to me and whispers in my ear, "Do you want to sit in the back of the room? This is for a grade."

"I think I'd like to try sitting here today," I answer. "You said for smaller assignments I don't have to move." Tony nods, then goes to his desk.

"Guess what?" I whisper to my quad as soon as Tony's gone. Max and Amy don't look up. They've already started writing. "I kicked a football into my bedroom window by accident. Now there's a hole in my wall where my window should be. I'm so miserable."

"Why are you miserable?" Trina asks. "A hole in your wall is the coolest thing I've ever heard. I would paint a bull's-eye around it. Or a giant eye."

"Well, my Dad nailed plywood over it until the repair guy comes. So now I have a windowless bedroom, like a dungeon."

Trina wiggles her fingers. "A dark lair. Excellent."

"Plus, I have to do homework at the kitchen table in front of my mother," I continue. "Being grounded is the worst."

"I've never been grounded before," Trina says. "What's that like?"

"Super fun. Early bedtime, no social media, no Netflix or sports until my homework is done . . . no . . ." My voice trails off. Max and Amy have stopped writing. They're listening, but something is off. There's a shift behind their eyes.

Amy doesn't play sports, Trina isn't on social media, and Max watches magic videos, not Netflix shows.

My grounded is their normal. I'm making them feel bad about themselves.

I'm in the midst of a conversational accident.

Change the subject. Fast. "It's not so bad. My brother smuggled in my mom's *Cosmopolitan* magazines. There was an article called 'Are Your Breasts Asymmetrical?'" I was horrified to learn, after staring at myself in the bathroom mirror for ten minutes, that yes, in fact, the little bit I have is totally asymmetrical. How did I not notice this hideous deformity before now?

Amy grins when I mention *Cosmo*. "Have you read that magazine?" I ask her.

She smiles. "Mm-hmm. My mom gets it too." We both break out into peals of laughter. Amy must know *Cosmo* is practically like watching an R-rated movie. It's the most inappropriate magazine ever. Judging from their baffled faces, Max and Trina have never seen it.

Who knew Amy and I could have an inside joke?

"You all need to get back to work," Tony says, looking over at us.

We whisper quieter. "Drew found all these back issues snooping through my mom's stuff," I say. "I read the articles, and he drools over the models in their underwear."

"Sounds right," Max says.

"Oh, and Drew found a bottle of Mom's perfume. Guess what it's called? *Sexy*." I pout my lips. We die laughing, quietly. "Can you imagine if your mom had a perfume called Sexy?" Max doesn't find that so funny. Maybe boys are more grossed out by that kind of stuff about their moms. He's back to writing his list of irony examples, but Trina, Amy, and I can't stop cracking up. Trina snort-laughs so loud, she sounds like a farm animal. It's hard to recover after that.

"Keep it down," Tony cautions us. "We have the test coming up, so if you finish early, start the study guide. Use your notes."

Amy works on the assignment. Trina stares off into the distance like she's in a trance, then starts writing.

I watch the three of them. I want to go back to talking and laughing. And then it hits me. Hanging out with these three is starting to make me look forward to coming to school every day.

"Ten minutes left," Tony informs us. He walks up to our quad and whispers to me, "You're distracted. Why don't you go in the back?"

I take my paper and pencil, go to my lone table, and get to work. It *is* easier to focus back there, facing away from everybody. Kelvin is at the other table in the corner. We glance at each other briefly, then get back to work.

❋

Abby Green
  Examples of Irony
  DEFINITION: Irony: (noun) When the literal meaning of something is the opposite of the intended meaning.

EXAMPLES:

I'm hyper, but I have to take a stimulant to calm down enough to focus. It's like going upstairs to get downstairs.

The older my mom gets, the younger she wants to look. She is dressing like a preschooler now. She has become Benjamin Button.

My grandparents own a business named Pewter Palace. It is not a palace. It is a flea-market stall the size of a Tic Tac box.

I'm coordinated on a field, track, or court, but somehow can't walk two feet without bumping into someone or spilling or breaking something.

My teacher thinks I should be a stand-up comic, but no one in my family thinks I'm funny except my brother Drew and my grandpa, and the only reason Grandpa laughs at my jokes is because I'm pretty sure I'm his favorite grandchild. (Although I have a sneaking suspicion he's telling Drew the same thing.)

80% B-

As much as I like your examples, I assigned eight, not five. Next time, a little less socializing will give you more time to get that A you deserve!

26

✳

Let's never speak of this again, and if you'll excuse me, I have to go fake my own death.

I can't wait to make them all fall out of their seats laughing. I didn't prepare anything, but how different can this be from joking around in class? They laugh at my material all the time.

I'm confident in my new star tank, dragon jeans, and red flip-flops. I skipped my medicine this morning on purpose, because I want to be my true self. It's not a written test. It's comedy.

I start, pacing back and forth in front of my audience. "Why do we have to take English? Don't we already know English? We should all automatically get As." I'm pacing too fast. I slow down, the way comedians do on TV. "So they make us take English and then what are we forced to study? Shakespeare! WHICH ISN'T EVEN ENGLISH. 'Tis a whol*eth* other*eth* language, am I right*eth*?" I wait. Nothing. Quiet. I spot Sofia and her friends. Their first language isn't English. That joke couldn't have been funny to them. I should have thought about that.

I swallow nervously. "So when I first met Tony, he asked me, 'Have you ever read Shakespeare?' and I was like, 'I don't know, who wrote it?'"

Max laughs a little. So does Trina. But no one else.

What am I supposed to talk about up here? I'm not my sparkly self *at all*.

"Hello?" I whisper. "You guys are so quiet. It's as quiet as . . . as . . ." Amy's pretty face catches my eye. ". . . as quiet as *Amy* in here." Everyone whips their heads around to check out Amy, who looks down. "Amy is so quiet, the only way I can tell she's awake is if her eyes are open."

I meant that to be funny, but as soon as the words come out, I hear how mean they sound. Super mean. Amy hangs her head even lower.

That was horrible of me.

Embarrassment dries up my throat. I stop looking at faces and instead limit my gaze to the tops of people's heads. I don't want to see the way they're looking at me. Or worse, tuning out entirely, like Sofia. She's been secretly texting the whole time using a stack of books to block Tony's view.

I pick up a glass paperweight sitting on Tony's desk. "Tony, why do you have a paperweight? What are you expecting, a freak storm to blow the windows open and let in wind that will blow your papers away into the stratosphere? What good are paperweights *inside*? Wind doesn't happen *inside*!"

Tony smiles. Doesn't laugh. Just smiles.

Sofia yawns. Long and loud. The yawn travels around the room contagiously, striking one person after the other.

I feel like I'm trapped in a car with no air. This is a nightmare. I'm bombing. I wouldn't be surprised if they threw their water bottles and sodas at me.

Why did I think I could perform without a script, unprepared? *Why can't I make them laugh easily, without thinking, the way I do during class?*

Brrrrrrrrrrrrrring. The bell goes off. So does most of the class. And so do I.

"Abby!" Tony calls after me. I keep going.

Max, Trina, and Silent Amy catch up with me outside. "You all right?" Max asks.

"You weren't that bad," Trina says immediately, which, of course, means I was.

"Yeah," Amy whispers.

"Is that supposed to make me feel better?" I ask, mortified.

"You need practice, that's all," Max says, like my father says to Drew in the backyard even though everyone knows it's a lost cause. "You got better toward the end."

Amy nods. How can she be nice to me after what I said about her? "I didn't mean to single you out," I tell her. "Well, I guess I did, but I'm sorry about how it sounded. I was . . . trying to come up with something better, but I couldn't."

"'S okay," she says. If I were her, I would want to kill me. I take a good look at her. There's a sweetness in her face I'm just now seeing. "They were jokes," she whispers.

Max and Trina start talking over each other in an attempt to comfort me, about how every comedian or actor bombs sometimes, and how I should keep working at it. Max ends his pep talk with, "You'll get plenty of practice working a crowd at my magic shows. Then you'll be ready for this."

"Truth," Trina says. "You just need some experience, and you'll be *fierce*."

"I already had enough of an experience today, thanks," I say.

"You're supposed to learn something from this, that's all," she says. *Yeah, I'm learning I'm not as good as I thought I was.*

Mom's car pulls up to the curb. "Let's never speak of this again and if you'll excuse me, I have to go fake my own death. It was nice knowing you."

"What happened?" Mom asks when I get in. "Are you okay?"

"Nothing happened. I just tried to do a little comedy routine, and it wasn't funny. I'm fine."

"Oh, Abbles. I'm sorry." She asks a few more questions.

"Mom, leave me alone. *Please!*"

"I'm just trying to help."

"I don't need your help." Guilt, guilt, guilt. "Sorry, I didn't mean that."

I'm pretty stunned by what Mom does next, which is to pull in to a McDonald's drive-through and get me a chocolate milk shake. She never gives me junk food. "When I was your age and had a bad day, Grandma bought me a milk shake."

"But it has sugar."

"We can make an exception today."

Who is this alien in the form of my mother? "Thanks, Mom." I put on my headphones, stare out the window, and slurp my shake. It doesn't make me feel better.

Why didn't my performance turn out the way I imagined it? I stank. Badly. I didn't even do any of my characters or accents. I thought today would be like goofing on the teacher or joking back and forth with someone in class, but up there by myself, it was different. My ideas didn't flow.

Maybe I'm even less talented than Caitlin. Maybe I'm not funny enough to do stand-up or be a professional actress. *The Abby Show* will never happen.

Have I been lying to myself about having something special inside me?

If I don't have that spark inside me, then I don't have anything unique going for me. My brain is just like a dog off its leash, wandering off the sidewalk.

Maybe I'm just an average troublemaker, another underachieving class clown.

Average.

I have to be more than that.

I *have* to be.

27

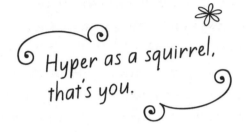

Hyper as a squirrel, that's you.

Everything I do lately is a disaster. My comedy debut is just one more failure to add to my list. I could have gotten an A on that irony assignment. Max and Amy got hundreds. (Trina got a seventy, but she doesn't try, and I don't think she cares.) I'm so tired of messing up. I want to ace our big test, get it right for a change.

Max suggests we all do a group study session. We meet at Dunkin' Donuts. It's our first time getting together outside of school. I just hope Max doesn't bring up me doing his magic show. I keep making excuses or changing the subject.

"Did you know soldiers in World War One were called doughboys because of all the doughnuts the volunteers gave them?" Max says with his mouth full. He likes glazed, same as me. "And did you know a squid's brain is shaped like a doughnut? They eat through the hole in it. If they swallow something too big, they get brain damage."

"Thank you, Captain Trivia." I lick crumbs off my fingers. "Why do squids even have brains?"

Trina practically downs her Very Berry smoothie in one slurp. "You're a fountain of information, Max. Where did you move from, Smartville?"

"Close," he says. "Pennsylvania."

"Oh, I love vampires," I say.

Amy scrunches her brows together, confused.

"That was a joke," I tell her.

She smiles like the Mona Lisa and takes a small sip of her orange smoothie. Sometimes I wonder about Amy. It doesn't seem like she's that smart, but she's a better student than the rest of us. Her notes and outlines are so good I'd pay for them. In fact, she gets the highest grades out of all of us: straight As. I can't figure out what on earth she's doing here.

It's the one thing none of us talk about. Why we all flunked.

"So what were you guys supposed to do on your summer vacation before we took this lovely detour?" I ask.

"Yoga and meditation camp," Trina says.

I make snoring sounds, fall over, and pretend I'm asleep. Then I pop back up.

Trina giggles. "My parents send me there to help me focus. I went last summer."

"ADHD?" I ask. She nods. I knew it.

"Like Abby," Max says.

"No, not exactly like Abby," Trina informs him.

"Right," I say. "There are different types."

It's obvious Trina has the non-hyper type most girls with ADHD have. Her mellow spaciness reminds me of Ivy Houseman, this girl on my soccer team. Ivy has ADHD but isn't on meds because she has a heart problem, so she can't take them. During games she was constantly wandering away from her position on the field and never knew where she was supposed to be.

"A doctor once told me the exact kind I have, but I don't remember," Trina says. "My parents told him they didn't believe in ADHD."

"Sounds like my Aunt Roz," I say. "She doesn't believe in it either."

"That's nuts," Max says. Amy nods, agreeing.

"My parents believe in it now," Trina says. "But they didn't at first. They think food, yoga, meditation, and natural remedies are very important. I'm not supposed to eat meat, eggs, preservatives, food coloring, or processed sugar."

"How's that working out for you?" I ask. Trina's got the worst case of LaLa Land I've ever seen.

"It *does* help," Trina says. "I don't get upset or anxious like I used to, and I sleep better. But I think my parents might finally be considering giving medication a try. They've never even filled out an IEP for school." That explains why Trina doesn't join Kelvin and me at the back tables for tests, or get offered extra time.

"Do *you* believe in ADHD?" Max asks her.

"Of course," she answers, holding her cup upside down over her open mouth so the last drops of her smoothie fall in. "I showed my parents this article about scientific proof of attention deficit. It had pictures of how ADHD brains are different and interviews with researchers about genes linked to it. That's when they started to change their minds. That and me flunking English." Trina puts her feet on her chair and hugs her knees. "I wasn't even upset when I found out I was going to summer school. It was the start of a new path, you know? And I got to know you guys." She grins.

Her words from that first day come back to me: *The universe is, like, always surprising us with a new path.* I didn't understand what she meant then, but I do now. Trina may be the most positive person I know. Who else could take a crappy situation like summer school and turn it into a good thing?

"My mom kicked Aunt Roz out of the house because she didn't believe in ADHD," I say.

"I wouldn't mess with your mom," Max says. I bet he's remembering that day in Publix when Mom terrorized the cashier. "What happened?"

"She was visiting us from New York. I was in fourth grade, just diagnosed, and she told my mother ADHD was fake. I went, 'Stop saying that! It IS real.' Something snapped inside me, like the night I redecorated Finsecker's neighbor's car. I threw a glass at the wall. Then Aunt Roz goes, 'See? What she needs is discipline.' Mom gave her the boot and she flew back to New York that day."

"Wow, your mom really stood up for you," Max says. There's something in his voice I haven't heard before. A hard edge.

"Yeah," Amy whispers. "She did."

I never thought about that before, about my mom sticking up for me. Aren't moms supposed to do that?

Max waves his hand in front of Trina's face. "Earth to Trina."

Trina is tracing the outline of her hand with her straw, using the napkin as paper. She looks up. "What?"

"How did you like my story?" I ask her.

She blinks at us.

"You might want to try taking those meds," I say. "Just a suggestion."

"Do they work for you?" she asks.

I take a second to think of the best way to describe it. "The medicine makes me sit. I can concentrate on one thing and get work done. Grown-ups tell me it works like a cup of coffee for regular people."

"Maybe I should try coffee," Trina says. "Not you, though, Abs. Hyper as a squirrel, that's you."

"Yup," I say. "When I'm off meds, it's like I'm zooming on a roller coaster *all the time.*"

"That sounds fun," says Max. "I love roller coasters."

"Me too, but it's not fun in school, believe me. *You* try writing an essay on a roller coaster. Meds help me get off the ride for a while. I only take them for school, not on weekends, because I don't have to sit all day on a weekend, unless I have a lot of homework. Plus, I eat better on the weekends when I'm off meds."

We all eat and sip, enjoying our snacks. After a while, I add, "My mom only let me come today because we're supposed to study."

"My mother couldn't care less where I am," says Trina. "She doesn't notice what I do."

"I'd give anything for a mother who doesn't notice what I do," I say.

"My mother left me and my dad last year," Max says. Trina stops chewing. Silent Amy stops sipping. "She found her high school boyfriend online and took off to go live with him and his son. Traded us in. That's why my dad took the job offer out here. He says it's because he's making more money, but I don't believe that."

"What do you believe?" Trina asks.

Max shrugs. "I think he just couldn't deal with living where everybody knew what Mom did. My hometown is small. People talk, you know?" We nod, stunned. "I never wanted to move."

"That's terrible" is all I can think of to say. "I'm so sorry, Max." For once, I'm saying I'm sorry and it's not for something I've done.

"It's supposed to be a secret, but I trust you guys. My dad doesn't want anyone to know. I don't even know if my parents are officially divorced yet. Dad won't talk about it. I haven't heard from Mom in months."

"That must be tough," says Trina.

"It is sometimes," says Max. "Like when I hear you all talking about your moms."

Complaining about our moms. That's what he really means.

Amy surprises all of us by reaching across the table and squeezing Max's hand. It seems like something an adult would do, but it's not weird, somehow, when Amy does it. She's not good with words, so she shows she cares with gestures. We get it.

"It's okay," Max says. "I didn't mean to be a downer. I used to be a real downer when it first happened, but

I'm better now." His light brown eyes are so sad and sweet, I have to look away.

No one is eating anymore. There's so much I want to ask him, like if he'll ever forgive his mom and if his dad has a girlfriend and are there still framed photos of his mom in his house?

Max pulls his outline out of his shorts' pocket and slaps it on the table. "If this is supposed to be a study session, maybe we should do some actual studying."

He's right. We all take out our notes and start filling out our study guides. Actually, Trina and I can't find ours, so we look at Amy's paper. Same thing.

28

I stink, remember?

I'M ALLOWED TO WATCH NETFLIX AGAIN!!!!!

Sort of.

I got a ninety on my Shakespeare chapter test. A NINETY! So I'm allowed to watch it, but only in the family room. My bedtime is still nine o'clock, but I've gotten Mom and Dad to drag it to nine-thirty on weekends. So things are looking up.

Drew and I are in the family room eating popcorn and watching a Netflix reality show called *100 Strange and Unusual Things Removed from Human Bodies*. This man had fifty-three toothbrushes in his stomach. Mom, Beth, and Grandma are talking while eating salads at the table next to the sofa.

"Bloomingdale's has the best baby department," Mom announces as if she's an expert.

"You need to find out which baby bottles have the best nipples," Grandma says.

Drew and I pretend to barf all over each other.

"Oh, no, I plan to breastfeed," says Beth.

I stick popcorn in my ears and whisper to Drew, "It's bad enough we have to hear about your bore mitzvah, now we have to hear baby this and baby that."

Beth winks at me. Earlier, she let me touch her belly, but there's no kicking yet. It makes me feel special, knowing I'm one of the few people who knows her secret about being overweight when she was younger.

Max has been on my mind a lot since he told us his secret. I don't blame him for being into magic or spouting off kooky trivia or being a little different. After your mother ditches you, you're probably going to feel different from everyone else no matter what you do.

Drew munches away, watching the gruesome surgical scene. He has no problem eating or drinking during gross TV programs. Yesterday he ate pizza while watching a documentary on diseases of the human skin.

My cell rings. Mom jerks her head toward it on the kitchen counter like a bloodhound smelling a fresh scent. With Caitlin gone, I never get phone calls. Mom gets up and walks over to the kitchen counter, then reads my phone screen. "Who's Max?"

"Ooh, a boy," Grandma says, raising her penciled eyebrows up and down. "Is he Jewish?"

I snatch my phone off the counter and answer, "Hey, I was just thinking about you."

Oh, no. That sounded as if I *like* him or something.

It doesn't help when Grandma goes, "She was *thinking* about him," again with the eyebrow action.

"Hang on a sec," I tell Max, zipping to the stairs. "What's up?" I ask, closing my bedroom door.

"I just wanted to remind you about my show to-morrow," he says. "My dad said he could give you a ride. Can you be ready at one?"

"For your show," I confirm, as though I don't speak English.

"Yes, for my show. We need to make a stop first, so you'll—"

"Max, I can't . . ." I bite my lip until it hurts. "I can't do it. I can't."

No sound from Max's end.

"Are you there?"

"Why can't you do it?" His voice is flat. Angry.

Because there is no way I'm making a fool of myself again, especially in a public place.

172

"What are you so afraid of, Abby?" His voice is back to normal.

"I'm not afraid of anything, but it's not like doing magic with you at a Home Depot opening will give me a head start on my future, you know?"

Silence. Oh, man, I did it again.

"It's not at a Home Depot opening, it's at Millennium Lakes." Then he goes, "You know what, Abby Green? You are a snob."

Beep. He hung up on me.

Oh, no way, Max Finkelstein. I press CALL BACK.

Instead of saying hello, he answers, "You think you're too good to perform with me. Too cool or something."

"What?! I'm far from cool. Haven't you noticed I only have one good friend in regular school? And she treats me like garbage, by the way." I can't believe I just admitted that to him.

"Ooh, I don't know if there's room for me in your life of glitz and glamour," he mimics. "At least I'm putting myself out there, taking a chance. You talk about wanting to be famous, but look at you. You're not doing anything about it."

"I am too. I tried to do stand-up for Tony's class. It was a ginormous disaster. I stink, remember?"

"So that's it? You're never going to try again?"

"Probably not."

"Well, that's stupid. And chicken."

173

My breath catches in my throat. "I don't think I'm too cool for you. You're my friend, you dork."

"Then why won't you do a gig for me as a friend?"

I have no answer to that. A good friend would do it for him. "Don't call it a gig. Gigs are when you get paid. Volunteering at an old-age home is not a gig."

"You know what, Abby? You say things that are *unbelievably* rude, and you never know when to keep your mouth shut. You're always fidgeting, running, talking a mile a minute! You're a pain! An exhausting pain!"

"*You're* an exhausting pain too!" I shout. This time I hang up on him. He thinks *I'm* exhausting? Max Finkelstein is the most exhausting person I know. He's constantly pestering me about being in his magic shows, never letting it go. I hug myself, stinging inside.

"Abby!" Mom calls from downstairs. "Please come down and clean up your mess! There's popcorn all over the couch where you were sitting! I am not your maid!"

Actually, there is one other person who might be more exhausting.

29

*Pretty?
I've seen better
heads on lettuce.*

Yet another excellent Saturday. I was helping Dad at the store when I accidentally tipped over the bin of soccer balls, which messed up the display of golf clubs and a few other things. Dad went bonkers. I'm not allowed to work there anymore. So now I'm at Pewter Palace, my grandparents' indoor flea-market stall.

Maybe I was extra clumsy because I'm overtired. I tossed and turned all night because of my fight with Max. *You're a pain! An exhausting pain!* I'm so sick of criticism, of goofing up, of being me. I was just being honest about his dorky magic shows. At least I told him the truth. I'm not lying like I sometimes used to.

My grandparents gave me a few jobs to do, like wiping down all the serving platters and picture frames with some kind of spray, but Grandma complained that I used too much and made a mess, so then I started rearranging the displays and entertaining myself by popping open the cash register over and over. Grandpa finally just asked me to sit near the entrance and "look pretty."

Max is on my mind. *You talk about wanting to be famous, but look at you. You're not doing anything about it. Snob.* I wouldn't help him now if he paid me a billion dollars. Even if he calls me to apologize, I won't answer. I have nothing to say to him.

I called Trina after my fight with Max. It felt good to talk to her out of school. We call each other all the time now. She thinks Max likes me as more than a friend. "Why else would he still be friends with you after you insulted him in class and made fun of his magician career?" I told her she's dead wrong, and it doesn't matter anyway because I don't like him that way. "Really? Because you talk about him all the time" was her answer. I do not!!!

"Hey, Grandma, what attracted you to Grandpa?" I ask.

"She couldn't resist my charms," Grandpa says, before honking into his handkerchief. Is there anything more disgusting than blowing boogers into a piece of cloth, sticking it in your pocket so it can get nice and soggy, then taking it out later to add more nose butter to it? No, there is not.

"Solly, do you have to blow so loud? You sound like a foghorn," Grandma says. Then, to me, she says, "I knew your grandfather had class the minute I met him. That's what attracted me."

"Really?" Grandpa and I ask at the same time. I find this hard to believe. Family lore has it they met when Grandma slipped on a fallen orange peel at the fruit stand where he worked. This prompted Grandpa's father, who owned the fruit stand, to say, "Solly, help the pretty girl up," and Grandpa replied, "Pretty? I've seen better heads on lettuce."

"How did you know he had class?" I asked.

"He offered me a white hanky to dab the juice stain off my blouse," Grandma says. "A clean, white hanky. That's class." Okay, so logic doesn't exactly run in my family. But it does explain Grandma being okay with Grandpa's gross handkerchief habit. "And look at us now," Grandma coos. "Fifty-four years later."

"Don't remind me," Grandpa says. "I walked her home that day. My father said, 'What do you have to lose? Give it a shot.'"

My phone rings. It's Max!

I step outside the stall. "I've decided I'll try a show with you," I hear myself say.

Wait. What did I just say?

"I'm sorry I said those things to you," Max replies. "You do have friends. Me, for example. Which proves you're definitely not a snob."

"Apology accepted. I'm at the Carnival Indoor Flea Market, by the way."

"Really? I'm on my way there."

"No way."

"Way. Meet me at the food court."

＊

Max is easy to spot at Wok on the Wild Side. My heart leaps when I see him. I don't know why. I should still be a little bit mad. "In China they serve turtle soup and snake," he says, slurping up a noodle.

"Did you come to this flea market for the Chinese food? Or just to see me?"

"I came for the props at the joke-supply stall. You can help me pick some out, because you're doing a show with me at Millennium Lakes in two hours."

"Today?"

"Don't worry. Since it's your first time, you can just watch, get a feel for it." He's excited, energized. It's like our argument never happened. We're back to normal.

"How can I? I'm working at my grandparents' stall."

He leans across the table toward me, lowering his

voice as if revealing information vital to homeland security. "Tell your grandparents we have to write a paper due Monday. They can't say no if it's for school. You owe me. You probably would have gotten arrested, losing an old man in a tree trunk."

Something about the phrase *losing an old man in a tree trunk* makes us both laugh. "Probably," I admit. "But if I get caught lying and skipping work, my life is over. I can't lose Netflix again. That's a big thing with me."

"Come on, it's not like you're going to a party. What's the harm in leaving here to do a good deed? You're cheering up old people. Actually, just tell them the truth—you're volunteering. You're supposed to be doing that anyway."

He's right. Plus, it's a good deed, a *mitzvah*. It would actually be an act of kindness to ditch this place and watch Max's show.

"You won't be sawing me in half today or anything, right?" I ask.

"No, but I do have this box I can put on your head and poke knives through it all around your face."

"That sounds better than working at Pewter Palace. Let's get to that joke-shop stall," I say. "We only have two hours."

But I have to tell Grandma and Grandpa first.

30

At least if I fail, most of these people won't remember me tomorrow morning. Some won't remember me in ten minutes.

Grandma and Grandpa didn't question me when I told them I had to leave with Max to do community service at Millennium Lakes. They gave me fifty dollars for my five hours and said they'd see me next weekend. It was like they couldn't get me out of there fast enough. Grandpa slipped me another ten when Grandma wasn't looking.

Max's dad gives us a ride and doesn't say one word in the car except "hello" to me and "don't forget your prop case" to Max. Whenever I have a friend in the car, my mother interrogates them like Sherlock Holmes until she practically finds out their blood type, or at least what their parents do for a living.

Once we arrive, Max starts setting up props in the rec room, next to the platters of cookies and juice. I help myself to a cookie. If it makes me a little hyper for the performance, all the better. Hyper is probably a good thing for a magic show.

The chairs are nailed to the floor, which doesn't make any sense because why would the patients who live here want to steal chairs? It's not like they have houses to put them in at this point. I share my thoughts on this with Max, but he's not listening. He's smoothing a black tablecloth over a table. Then he arranges oversized cards, multicolored handkerchiefs, metal rings, an orange, carrots, and a few other bizarre props. His big black prop case fits neatly under the table.

I've always wondered how those metal rings work. I swing them around, trying to figure out how they separate, but wind up bonking myself in the head. Max yanks them out of my hand and lays them out on the table with the care of a surgeon laying out his instruments before operating. "Can you stop touching everything?" he asks.

"I can't help it. I love touching things."

"That's not even a real pack of gum. It shoots water."

I open it and squirt myself in the face.

Max turns his attention to plugging in his micro-phone. I plunk down on a chair behind him and observe him tying on his black cape and putting on a top hat.

I tell him his hat looks dumb.

"What?"

"I'm just saying. Are you hiding a prop in it?"

"What do you think I am? That is so amateur."

"Then take it off. Have you seen Criss Angel? He makes magic look cool because his hair flies free."

"I didn't ask you for your opinion." But he takes off the hat.

Bonnie, the activities director, comes in while Max finishes setting up. "Mr. Meyers asked me to take pictures for our newsletter and website." She holds up her phone. "Is that okay with the two of you?"

"Sure," I tell her, getting an idea. "Would you mind taking a video too? And then you could text it to me?"

"Great idea," she says. "I'd be happy to."

The residents are rolling in now. And I do mean rolling, as in wheeled walkers and wheelchairs. Nurses and recreational therapists come in too. It makes me realize how lucky I am that my grand-parents aren't super old. They're just a little bit old.

I keep looking for Simon, and, finally, I spot his bushy gray eyebrows. He stops his wheelchair right in front of me. "Hello there, Abby! Do you play chess?"

"Of course," I say. I've never played chess in my life.

He points in my face and goes, "Good. It's your move. GET OUTTA DA WAY!" Then he laughs until he wheezes, turns his wheels like a maniac, and practically runs me over.

Max taps the mic a few times to make sure it's working. "Hello, everyone, I'm Max Finkelstein, and I've got a great show for you today." He sounds as excited as Mom announcing dinner's ready. "Okay, well, uh . . . let's get on with the show." Then he clears his throat about fifty times. I'm going to have to work with him on his stage presence.

He puts down the mic and picks a few people from the audience for some "pick a card, any card" tricks. Since the residents can't get up so easily, Max goes to them. They clap every time he guesses their card correctly, but their clapping sounds like drizzling raindrops. Slow, without energy. Max does a few more tricks using cups and paper clips. It's dead in here.

"Can I get a volunteer?" Max asks. "Anyone?" Yawning silence. "Anyone?" he begs. Finally, a lady gets up, grabs onto her walker, and slowly makes her way toward Max. Thank God. Audience participation. Success.

But no. She shuffles past Max and keeps going, heading for the door, inch . . . by . . . inch. Max tries to ignore her and go on with his act, but the lady is taking about nine years to get across the room. The worst part is that the lady's walker is making this squeaking noise with every move, like a rusty shopping cart. *Squeak,* step. *Squeak,* step. *Squeak,* step. If I were Max, I would climb inside the prop case and hide.

When the walker lady is finally gone, Max starts with the metal rings. He's juggling, separating, and connecting them. This gets some light applause. It's going okay until he drops them. *Clang! Ping! Pang!* One of the old-timers covers his ears. Some of them are asleep. Poor Max.

I scramble around on the floor and pick up the rolling metal rings. Max is sweating, wiping his brow with his sleeve. Now he takes out a metal box, setting up another trick, but he stops to pick up the microphone on the table and say, "Technical difficulties, folks. It'll just take a second." He places the mic back down. The chairs creak. The air-conditioning hums.

I make a decision. Max needs my help. I lay the metal rings down, take the mic off the table. "How's everybody doing today?" I ask brightly.

Somebody coughs. Max is still messing around with the metal box.

I tap on the mic. "Hello? Hello? Are you all still alive? Do I need to do CPR on anybody?"

Max grins at me encouragingly. At least if I fail, most of these people won't remember me tomorrow morning. Some won't remember me in ten minutes.

I scan the room for a victim. I spot Simon. Perfect. I go over to him, take his wrist, and feel his pulse.

"How's my blood pressure?" he asks, playing along.

"I have no idea. I'm just making sure you're still alive." Simon clutches his heart, as if he's having a heart attack. A few people laugh.

Someone is snoring. I scan the room and see that the snorer is a very thin, sickly-looking old-timer. He's out cold. I hold my microphone up to the man's mouth, amplifying his snores: *pishrrrrchhhssshh, pishrrrrccchhhhsssh.* "Is there a helicopter landing in here?" I ask.

Now they're cracking up. One old guy's head is so shiny I pretend it's a mirror while I stare into it and put my lip gloss on. I polish it with a handkerchief. It's a stupid joke, but even the nurses laugh. I may have tanked in front of my classmates, but I'm killing it with these senior citizens.

Max starts rummaging around in his prop case, so I stand behind him and say in this low, educational-documentary-type voice, "Look, ladies and gentlemen, a young nerd, scrounging for food! Let's see what he finds, nuts . . . berries . . . computer parts . . . a Spider-Man mask . . . a spelling bee trophy . . ."

Max stands up and pulls out a three-sided box with mirrored insides. He faces all the old people. "Uh," he says, "thank you all for being such a great audience. Let's, um, hear it for the comedy stylings of my very entertaining assistant, Abby Green." They clap. "Uh . . . and now for the grand finale, the moment you've all been waiting for." He slips the box over my head. The front is open so I can look out.

Max whips out an electric drill. "This will only take a minute." Then he whispers, "Just play along. Pretend the screws are hurting you and *make sure* the back of your head is touching the back of the box at all times. Keep your head at the back. Got it?"

"Wait, there are screws *and* a drill involved in this trick?" The drill is incredibly loud, and Max makes a big deal out of drilling these screws into the box. I'm freaking out, but I shout "ouch!" and "ack!" I don't know what he's going to do to me. I'm assuming it's all for show and not truly dangerous.

Until Max takes out knives.

KNIVES!!!

I thought he was kidding about the knife thing. What have I gotten myself into?

Max has Simon feel the tip of the knife with his fingertip to make sure it isn't a fake. "It's sharp, all right," Simon confirms. Then Max goes one step further, demonstrating its sharpness by slicing an orange in half.

It truly is a very sharp knife. And Max is coming toward me with it. He stands next to me, tosses his cape behind one shoulder with a flourish, and raises the knife high.

And thrusts it right into the side of my head.

Well, into the side of the box.

Thwack.

A blade springs out in front of my eyes. The audience gasps.

My heartbeat is pounding. "What the?" I rage-whisper to Max. "I didn't sign up for this. Get me out of this thing."

"Relax, they're trick knives," Max whispers out of the side of his mouth. "When I stab the box, the blade retracts into the handle. The blades that are popping out in front of you are soft plastic. They're inside the walls of the box. Make jokes."

So I shout, "Thanks, I was due for an eyebrow trim!" after the next blade springs out in front of me. I point at Simon's bushy eyebrows. "You're next, Simon, you really need it." Laughter fills the room. It's louder now, there's energy.

Max raises his hand, poises the knife, and *throws it at my head. THWACK.*

The knife lands in the hidden slot on the box. *Whew.*

Suddenly, I realize that Max had it right all along. This *is* fun. And I'm great at it. Why did I resist for so long?

Max's finale is inserting a bunch of knives in the box super-duper fast while more fake blades criss-cross and pop out. I wince with every *thwack.* The effect is probably scary because the inside of the box is mirrored, and I'm sure it looks like more knives than it really is. At the end, Max pulls out the fake knives, then carefully removes the back wall of the box so I can get my head out of it, and takes my hand. We bow together to pretty decent applause.

It doesn't feel weird that he's holding my hand. It's professional, like a curtain call. "I knew you could do it," he says, dropping my hand.

As the audience rolls toward the cookies and juice, Simon calls out, "Great job, you two."

"Thanks, Simon," we say. I add, "I look forward to seeing you next weekend!"

I mean it. Right now, Simon Eppelmeyer is the most adorable little old guy in the universe. So what if tiny balls of white spittle collect in the corners of his mouth, like little saliva Q-tips? The poor man just needs a glass of water.

People should be more sensitive toward old-timers, like I am.

Bonnie comes up to us and says, "You two were terrific." She holds up her phone. "I'll send the pictures and video to you, Abby."

Max looks down at me. I finally did something right. So did he. We both accomplished something special today. I know he feels it too.

31

Keep dreaming. My grandpa gives me that for scratching his back.

I'm bursting with ideas: a website, maybe a local news interview, social media advertising, marketing videos, plus a special YouTube-project surprise for Max. I can't wait to get started. Being Max's assistant *is* performing experience, for both comedy and acting. Who cares what Caitlin or anyone else thinks? I think it's cool.

And when I picture the laughing, wrinkly faces of the Millennium Lakes residents (the ones who were awake), and their smiles (the ones with their teeth in), I feel pretty good about myself. Max and I put those smiles on their faces. We brought a room to life, entertained them.

Maybe I *do* have talent, after all.

At school, I wait for Max outside before class starts. As soon as he gets out of his dad's car, I pounce. "My brother Drew said he'd film us for promotional videos. Plus, you need to be active on our social media sites. We've got major work to do."

"Abby—"

"I was thinking you could mess up a few tricks and then I could do them and get it right, you know, like we pretend the assistant knows more than the magician?"

"Abby—"

"And there's this dress I think would be perfect if my mom will give in and buy it for my brother's bar mitzvah, and—"

"Abby, stop interrupting me!"

"Sorry."

"We have a gig this weekend. As in money."

"Really?! What is it?"

"A kid's birthday party."

"Whaaaat? Awesome! How much?"

He grins. "A hundred dollars."

"Wow!" A second later I remember I'm his partner. "I'm getting fifty."

"Twenty-five."

"Keep dreaming. My grandpa gives me that for scratching his back."

"Thirty-five."

"Forty."

"Deal."

We shake on it and go to class. I'm making money to perform for people!

It feels right.

❋

Later, we're all outside at our picnic table, copying Amy's study guide. If we show a study guide for our quiz this afternoon, we get five extra points. "Amy, I don't know how you got a bad grade in English," I tell her. "Your outlines are awesome." Although the rest of us probably should start doing our own at some point.

Trina doodles in the margins of her outline. "Yeah, you're such a good student. How *did* you flunk?"

"I didn't," Amy says.

"What do you mean, you didn't?" Trina asks. "Why are you here?"

Silent Amy thinks for a few seconds, smoothes out her skirt. "I got a D, not an F, but my parents still made me come. Mr. Finsecker was way too hard for me. I didn't keep up with the work. I didn't outline or study like I'm doing now. I didn't understand Mr. Finsecker most of the time, so I didn't try. So that's how I got a bad grade, I guess."

Trina, Max, and I gape at her. For Silent Amy, that was the equivalent of Abe Lincoln's "four score and seven years ago."

"I've never heard so many words come out of your mouth at one time," I say.

Amy bursts into tears.

"I'm so sorry," I backpedal. "Did I say something wrong?" I hug her, because I don't know what else to do. She smells like a vanilla candle. "Don't cry. You surprised us, that's all. Conversation isn't your thing. I'm sorry for what I said."

"No, it's n-not that," she sobs. Naturally, we all ask her what's wrong.

"I'm not good with people. I don't know what to say to them," she sniffles. "I never know what to say. That's why I don't have friends."

Max, Trina, and I look at each other, bewildered. "Amy, *we're* your friends," I assure her. "Aren't we?"

"Definitely," Max says.

"Of course," Trina adds.

I hug her again. "We don't care that you're quiet. I kind of like it. The rest of us can't shut up, right, guys?"

"Truth," Trina says, putting her arm around Amy. "Especially you, Abby."

"Yeah," Max agrees.

I scowl at both of them.

Trina gives Amy's hand a squeeze, like Amy did for Max. "Maybe you just need to relax. Then you'll know what to say. It's just us."

Amy sniffs, shakes her head. "It's not you. It's me. I just . . ." She shrugs, sobs. "I never know what to say. I can never think of anything." She looks at each of us. "That sounds crazy, right?"

"Not crazy," I say. "My brother Drew is like that." Really, Drew doesn't seem to be that interested in connecting with people. Amy wants to, but can't.

The last thing I ever thought I would feel for Amy is pity. But I do. I feel sorry for her. I've always lumped Amy in with the popular crowd because of the way she looks, but now that I think back on it, she was always alone whenever I saw her outside of class. I don't even know who she ate lunch with. I never once imagined that someone as picture-perfect as Amy didn't have friends.

I thought that was just me.

"You're all so fun and interesting," she says, still crying. "Abby, you always know exactly what to say to make everyone laugh."

"I don't," I tell her. "Sometimes I make people cry, like now. Or I make people furious. I apologize for my big mouth every day."

Amy sniffs. "And, Max, you're the best magician

193

I've ever seen. Trina, you've got your art. What do I have? Nothing. I'm nothing." Her voice is louder than I've ever heard it, raw with pain. Tears stream down her face. "I don't have a talent. I can't even *talk*." She crumples up into her own lap, sobbing.

Now it's Trina who hugs her. "You don't have to talk. Your vibe attracts your tribe. That's us. We're your tribe, and you are *not* nothing, Amy." Max and I nod. "I'm sure you *do* have a talent. Everyone does. You just don't know what it is yet."

"Right," Max puts in. "You're super organized and great with outlines. You dress like you came out of a magazine. You'll figure it out."

"And you *can* talk to people, Amy," I assure her. "You're talking to us right now."

She shakes her head like she doesn't believe any of us and wipes her nose and eyes with a napkin.

Maybe I can give her some advice. "There was this girl Totally Cindy on the Poco rec league soccer team—" I start.

"Totally Cindy?" Max repeats.

"Her real name was Cindy Miller," I explain. "I called her Totally Cindy in my mind because all she ever said was the word *totally*. Did you know you can say *totally* no matter what people are talking about?"

Amy sniffs. I take this to mean she wants me to keep going.

"Someone start a conversation with me," I say.

"Give me a random comment that isn't a question, but one where you'd expect an answer. Make something up." Max is suddenly busy texting back and forth with someone, not paying attention, which is pretty rude. Amy needs us. "Trina, you start."

"Abby, your parents don't understand the way things are," says Trina.

"Totally," I say, grateful she jumped in.

Silent Amy's puffy face has the beginnings of a smile. I point to our Shakespeare book. "This book stinks," I offer.

"Totally," she whispers.

"It is so hot outside," Trina says.

"Totally," Amy repeats.

"See?" I tell her. "It works."

"Totally," she whispers. Slowly, she smiles. "Thanks."

(There is no Totally Cindy. I made her up to make a point. But wouldn't she make a good character for *The Abby Show* someday? Totally.)

Max looks up from his phone. "Abby, could you stop shaking the picnic table?" His voice is sharp. He shoots me a nasty look.

I stop wiggling my foot. "I can't help it. It's more difficult for me to sit still than it is for most people."

"So try harder. I'm getting motion sickness," Max says, shoving my papers at me.

"What's your problem?" I shove the papers back toward him. What did I do?

"Your stuff is taking up the whole table," Max says, shoving them back at me. This time they fall onto the ground. He grabs his backpack and storms off, heading into the building.

Who was Max texting? Why did he get so mad at me?

Amy picks my papers up off the ground and hands them to me.

"Well, that came out of nowhere," Trina says.

"Totally," Amy says.

32

Something in his voice turns my knees into marshmallows.

I text, FaceTime, and call Max after school to find out what his issue is. He doesn't answer. Then, just before I get into bed, my phone beeps with a text. It's him.

Can u call me now?

I take my phone and go inside my closet to make sure no one can hear me. He picks up right away. "Why are you so angry?" I want to know. "What did I do?"

"I'm not. My dad sent me a text that really ticked

me off. I took it out on you. I'm sorry." He sounds stuffed up, like he's been crying.

"Shoving my papers off the table like that? Yelling at me for shaking the table? That was messed up, Max."

"I know."

"Remember when you made me promise not to embarrass you in front of people? You did the same thing today."

"Well, do you have to shake your foot all the time?"

"I don't know when I'm doing it. You don't have to make me feel bad about it."

He's silent for a moment. Then he says, "I'm really sorry."

Something in his voice turns my knees into marshmallows. "I forgive you. What did your dad's text say?"

He takes a long breath, blows it out. "He said he wasn't going to send me back to Pennsylvania to visit my mom. She wants to see me. He told her no."

"He told you that in a text?"

"That's my dad."

That's cold. "Now I get why you were so mad," I say. "Maybe she'll come here?"

"She can't. Not anytime soon. My father won't talk about it with me. He doesn't talk about anything with me."

"Your mom got in touch. That's good, right? It's a start. You'll see her soon."

"Yeah," he answers. We don't say anything for a few seconds. "Thanks for making me feel better. You cheer everyone up, like you did with Amy today. I wish I could be like you."

"No, you don't." *No one has ever wished they could be like me.* "Hey, I'm working on something that will really cheer you up."

"What is it?"

"It's a surprise."

"Listen, my dad will get mad if he hears me on the phone this late. I just wanted to say I'm sorry for the way I acted today. You are very messy, though."

"I know."

"Friends?"

"Definitely. Friends."

I work on my project for Max and wonder about how complicated his home life is, and the way Amy thinks she's nothing, and how Trina's in another world and her parents don't seem to care.

I thought I had problems. The truth is, I'm lucky.

❋

Class is always more fun when I get to read aloud. Today I get to read the part of this goofy guy named

Nick Bottom in *A Midsummer Night's Dream*, who thinks he's handsome and smart, only he's a big dummy because this fairy named Puck tricked him into wearing a donkey head. Tony pairs me with Max, who reads Quince, a guy who doesn't let Bottom know he looks ridiculous.

"'Ask me not what,'" I read, "'for if I tell you, I am no true Athenian. I will tell you everything, right as it fell out.'"

Max replies, "'Let us hear, sweet Bottom.'"

Kelvin makes a farting noise. "Did everyone hear that sweet bottom?"

The class explodes. Everyone thinks it's hilarious. Amazingly, I don't have the urge to join in. I wait for the snickering to wind down. "'No more words. Away, go away!'" I finish. Everyone claps.

"Abby, tell us why your character provides comic relief throughout the play," Tony asks.

"I don't know."

"Not acceptable," Tony responds. He never accepts "I don't know" for an answer. "I must say I'm surprised you're not laughing like so many of your classmates here."

"Nick Bottom isn't a funny character to me."

Tony sits on his desk. "Why?"

"Well, he walks around with this mask of a donkey stuck on his head, right?"

"Right."

"Only he doesn't know it, and the whole time, he thinks he's good-looking and important, when some of the others see him as this stupid donkey. They make fun of him behind his back because he's too stupid to know he's an idiot. Puck is mean." Tony nods, listening, so I keep going. "There's a difference between mean and funny. Sometimes a person doesn't know the difference." *Sometimes that person is me.* "Puck knows he's being mean."

As I say that, I realize Puck reminds me of someone.

"I've got a sister like that," says Kelvin.

I've got a friend like that. She's at Camp Star Lake.

"What do you think, Max?" Tony asks.

"I agree with Abby," he answers. "They're pranking him, and it isn't right. No one tells the guy he looks like a donkey. If they were true friends, they would."

Tony claps for us. "Well done, you two. Exceptional job of interpreting Shakespeare's intent. Abby, you have a strong stage presence, as always. You are both meant to have an audience. As for each of you."

Max and I grin at each other. I like the way his blue braces shine under the fluorescent lights.

It's a great feeling, standing out in class, and not for horsing around, for a change, but I can't stop rewinding the scene in my head. Am I like that guy Bottom? I mean, I could be walking around thinking

I've got something special and different inside me, that I'm destined for fame, and the whole time everyone is laughing behind my back, thinking I'm a dumb donkey.

That is a very disturbing possibility.

33

Is there a psycho killer leaving you threats on your closet door?

I asked Mom if I could invite friends over, and she said yes! I'm allowed to have them in my room as long as I keep the door open. My *friends*. Our unlikely summer school gang has officially become our very own clique. I've never been in one before. None of us has.

Seeing pretty, shiny Amy standing on my doorstep is unreal, like seeing a unicorn. I know she doesn't get invited anywhere, and neither do I. An everyday thing to most kids is a big deal to us. She could be thinking that too.

Trina comes next, wearing paint-splattered jeans

and socks with flip-flops. "Thanks for dressing up," I tell her.

She grins. "Just for you."

Mom takes one look at Trina and goes, "You must be Trina, the artist."

"Yes, hi," Trina says.

"Did you know there's a hole in your sock?" Mom asks, concerned.

"Oh, yeah, I know," Trina answers. She wiggles her toe.

The doorbell rings. It's Max, the last to arrive, carrying his laptop under his arm. It feels weird to have them all in my house, but good too.

My bedroom floor is the usual clutter of clothes, shoes, books, magazines, papers, and the occasional gum wrapper. I should have cleaned up. Trina plunks herself down and pulls a bottle of red nail polish out of her bag. She doesn't mind my messiness, and neither does Max. He sits next to her and opens his laptop.

But Amy is so sleek and put together in her halter top and jeweled sandals, I'm a little embarrassed. She sits stiffly on the edge of my unmade bed and opens the *Entertainment Weekly* lying there. "I have a bunch of those," I tell her, pulling a stack out from my bottom desk drawer. "You can have them. Lots of good celebrity gossip."

Amy hugs them to her chest. "Thank you." She kicks off her sandals, sits cross-legged on my bed, and starts reading.

Trina shakes her nail polish. "Check it out. I created this color by mixing five colors together."

Drew's voice suddenly sings out through my bedroom walls. *"Baruch atah Adonai . . . ,"* he chants.

Amy's eyes widen and dart around. Trina stops shaking the nail polish bottle.

"Your brother practicing for his bar mitzvah?" Max guesses.

"Yeah," I say. I yell at the wall. "Hey, Drew! Keep it down!"

Drew's answer is to barge in with his video camera, filming us.

Everybody waves. "Congrats, you're all in the bar mitzvah video," I tell them. "Okay, Drew, good-bye."

He puts down his camera. "Mom was supposed to take me to get my suit today, but she cancelled so your friends could come over. As usual, *you* come first."

"How can you say I come first?!" I shout. "It's been all about you and your stupid bar mitzvah for months!"

"Hey, kids, don't bite," Trina says. She pats the floor next to her. "Sit down, sibling." Drew sits down awkwardly. He doesn't say anything. "What do you think we should call this color?" she asks him.

Drew chews on his finger. "Internal Bleeding?" he suggests.

Her face glows. "You have a creative aura, Abby's brother."

"Hey, I have a question," Max says. "Is there a psycho killer leaving you threats on your closet door?" Max points to the note on my closet door written in heavy red marker:

TAKE YOUR MEDICINE OR ELSE!

"Because that," he says, "is freaky."

"I experiment with different ways of leaving myself reminder notes," I explain. "Otherwise, I forget my meds. I leave them in different places every couple of days. So far I haven't forgotten a dose since summer school started, so it's working."

"Wouldn't a note in the same place be better?" Max asks.

"No," I explain. "If it's in the same place, it becomes like wallpaper, and I don't see it after a while. I have to give myself the element of surprise, so I go, 'Ahhh! Take your meds.'"

"Where will you leave it next?" Trina wants to know.

"Hmm . . . inside my shoe, maybe?" I answer. "I haven't tried that yet."

"Smart," Amy says.

"Hi, everybody," Mom says, coming in with a bowl

of strawberries. She sets them down on the floor next to us. She's wearing short overalls with a tube top and sequined Converse sneakers. Not exactly the best look for a fifty-year-old with varicose veins. I introduce her to everyone, and she goes, "Quite the little breakfast club here."

I take a strawberry. "What do you mean by breakfast club?"

The Breakfast Club," Mom says, "is a movie from the eighties, about a bunch of kids in detention who become friends."

"That does sound like us," Trina says, and we all laugh, even Mom.

"I never watch anything from the nineteen hundreds," I say. "But if you guys want to watch it, I will."

"I'll get you the DVD," Mom says. "I recorded it from the Family Channel years ago, so there's nothing inappropriate. Anyone need anything? Chips? Popcorn?"

"Thanks, Mom. We're good." Mom leaves.

"Your mom is nice," Trina says.

"Right now she is, but sometimes, she's a real—" I stop talking, suddenly remembering about Max's mom. They're all looking at me, waiting for my answer. "Thanks. She is nice." Conversational accident avoided.

We all talk and eat strawberries. Mom brings us the DVD. We stay in my room and watch it on Max's laptop. I like how the kids are all so different, but they become super close. They aren't supposed to, but they do anyway.

In the movie, you can't tell if they'll stay good friends after they go back to school.

I wonder if we will.

34

For the most part, however, it's pretty much mass hysteria.

"Why did the toilet paper roll down the hill?" I ask the dozen little boys and girls sitting around me on the grass, wearing party hats and *Happy 5th Birthday, Logan!* buttons. It's a billion degrees in this park. I'll have to rethink this black, long-sleeved performance dress.

"Why did the toilet paper roll down the hill?" I repeat. A girl lies on her back and pulls her dress over her head, exposing *Sesame Street* underwear. I throw my hands up and shout, "To get to the bottom!" No laughs. "Get it? The toilet paper rolled down the hill *to get to the bottom.*" I get blank stares. We were so sure this would be a hit with little kids.

"Are you gonna paint my face?" Logan, the birthday boy, asks. "You're supposed to do face painting."

"I'm hot," another boy whines.

"Let's break out the carrot slicer," Max suggests quietly in my ear. The guillotine carrot slicer is a new trick Max and I picked out together. It works like this: when I stick my hand in it and Max pulls the fake guillotine down over my fingers, mini carrot slices pop out as I let out a scream. Then Max eats them. The guy in the joke shop said it's a guaranteed crowd-pleaser with little kids.

Max whips it out of the prop case with a big flourish and explains that his lovely assistant will put her fingers in it and magically survive the blade. I wiggle my fingers, slowly put them under the blade, and squeeze my eyes shut, making a frightened face.

Sesame Street underwear sits up. Logan leans forward, craning to see. Then Max says the line I told him to say: "I love lady fingers . . . for *lunch,* heh, heh, heh."

And—*SHWAK!*—the blade comes down.

"Aaaaaaaaaaaaahhhhhhhhhh!" I shriek as baby carrots fly out at the kids. Max scoops one up from the ground and bites into it.

Complete silence. And then Max's loud chomping.

Until one kid wails. And then another. Then another and another and another, until it goes viral and a bunch of them are scryming (screaming and crying). Only a few kids don't freak out. *Sesame Street* Girl is unfazed. She lies back down and waves her dress in the air. One boy eats carrots right off the grass until his father arrives and pulls them out of his mouth.

For the most part, however, it's pretty much mass hysteria. I don't get it. They're just carrots. Logan, the birthday boy, is the loudest crier of all. I pull my hand out of the contraption and show him my fingers, reassuring him it's a trick. The kid still freaks. His father picks him up, then shoots me and Max a look more sinister than the guillotine blade.

"What should we do?" I ask Max anxiously. He doesn't answer. He's busy tossing our props into his prop case at warp speed, not the slow, meticulous way he usually does. "What should we do?" I ask him again, avoiding angry looks from parents comforting their kids.

Logan's mother charges toward us. "Time to go," Max says, yanking me with one hand and hauling his prop case with the other.

"But we're supposed to do a half-hour show, and it's only been twenty minutes."

"What is the matter with you two, scaring little kids like that?" Logan's mom shouts, getting closer. I film her with my phone in case she tries anything.

"I thought you said you do children's birthday par-ties all the time," I say to Max as we break into a run.

"I didn't say I was good at it," he pants, his cape flying out behind him. "That's why you're here."

"GET BACK HERE! YOU'VE RUINED MY SON'S PARTY!"

"Wait up," I huff, stopping to pull off my heels for speed. I catch up to Max. "We really messed up this gig."

"Not totally," Max answers, dropping the case and picking it back up again. "I got paid in full before the party. Cash."

"Oh, good. Let's hit Smoothie Hut."

We pick up the pace, running faster and faster. Our laughter drowns out Logan's mom's shrieks. Soon we can't hear her at all.

When I get home, I look at the clips I filmed, plus the clips Bonnie sent me from our Millennium Lakes show. Drew filmed a show we did at the opening of a family restaurant, and one at an event outside Pet Supermarket.

I'm almost done transferring all the videos onto my computer. And then I can give Max his Big Surprise.

35

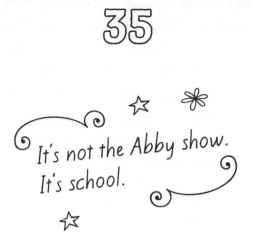

It's not the Abby show.
It's school.

Both my parents come to Dr. C's today. Dad is a space taker, filling up most of the couch he and I are sharing. Feet apart, legs spread open, his arm lying across the back. Mom is on a separate chair next to Dr. C's desk.

Dr. C swivels her chair to face my parents. "You know, ADHD often runs in families. One or both of you may meet some of the criteria yourself." Mom's eyes get wide.

"It's from your side, Rachel." Dad laughs. I giggle. Judging from the look Mom is giving him, she doesn't find this so funny.

"It doesn't matter which side," Dr. C says, holding her palms out as if she's surrendering. "I only bring it up because it's helpful if one or both parents can relate personally to what Abby is going through."

She swivels her chair back and types on her computer. "So, Abby, good job on remembering your meds. How's summer school? You seem a lot happier than the last time I saw you."

"I am. Summer school is better than I thought it would be."

"Why's that?"

"Um . . . I've made friends, and I'm performing in magic shows now. Oh, and my teacher's nice. I'm understanding the reading and keeping up. I don't call out in class as much as I used to, so Tony, he's my teacher, he let me perform a few minutes of stand-up comedy for the class."

"How did it go?" Dad asks, surprised.

"I bombed. I made fun of a friend, and it wasn't funny. I had to apologize later."

"You're still apologizing a lot, huh?" Dr. C asks.

"Yes," I admit. "Every single day, I say I'm sorry at least twice. That's 730 apologies a year. If I apologize three times a day, it's 1,095 apologies a year. My life is one long apology."

"Wow, that was some fast calculating," Dr. C says.

"Math is my thing."

Dr. C waves a pencil at my parents. "Imagine what

that feels like, having to apologize every day, multiple times. Try putting yourself in Abby's shoes."

My parents are quiet, thinking and searching my face. Then Mom says, "I never thought about how much you apologize for saying one thing or another. That's why people read you wrong when you accidentally say something insensitive, even though you're a sensitive person."

I lift my chin. "I am a sensitive person. That is why I am an actress."

Dr. C's manicured hands are poised over her laptop keyboard, and she's looking straight at me. "You said you're not calling out as much. But you're still calling out sometimes?"

"Not that often anymore, but when I do, the words are out of my mouth the instant I think them. Tony is helping me with that."

Mom shakes her head. "You can't disrupt a lesson with a song and dance every time you have a thought."

"I'm not singing or dancing," I tell her, feeling a knot of anger forming. It's like Mom is erasing all the good I've built up over the last few weeks. "What are you talking about?"

"Blurting is often involuntary, Mrs. Green, even on the medication," says Dr. C. "You have to remember that."

"I'm talking about calling attention to herself and

making jokes, *that* kind of song and dance," Mom says. "It's not the Abby show. It's school."

"But making jokes is the only way I get *through* school." My voice gets louder. "Besides, anywhere else, like in Hollywood or at Camp Star Lake, I'd be getting applause for cracking everyone up!"

Dr. C forms the *time out* sign with her hands. "Whoa, whoa, whoa. Abby, you're getting emotional. So are you, Mrs. Green. Abby won't confide in you if you do that. *Respond*, don't *react*, remember? Take a moment. You have both got to learn to control that angry, knee-jerk reaction that builds quickly into an argument. Let's hit the pause button before we continue."

I clamp my lips shut and stare at my knees. Dad shifts his feet and checks his watch. Mom hugs her purse on her lap. I decide we've had enough of a moment and say, "People are always telling me to calm down or stop interrupting or stop whatever. It's not easy when you're a spaz."

Mom points at me. "Don't say *spaz*. You are not."

"Yeah, I don't like that word either," says Dad. "Unless it's about Frank Spaziani, the football coach, also known as Spaz." Dad and I crack up.

The dead serious look on Dr. C's face stops us cold. "Let's stay on topic, okay?" She shifts her eyes to Mom. "It's important to listen and validate Abby's feelings, rather than constantly correct her."

216

"But I have to teach her," Mom insists. "She can't go around calling herself a spaz."

"Why not, if that's how she feels?" says Dr. C. "You have to listen when she's letting you in, not judge. Sometimes the best way to effect change is to just . . . listen."

"But—" Mom starts.

Dr. C interrupts her. "It sounds like you two need some quality mother-daughter bonding time. Try to listen and communicate with each other."

"No father-daughter time?" Dad asks.

"I sense you two spend plenty of time together and communicate well," Dr. C tells him. Dad gives me a smile.

"I offered to take Abby to the mall with me," Mom says. Her face is all pinched up. "I'd love some mother-daughter time. She's not interested."

"I am interested," I say. "But you won't let me get the dress I want, or color my hair blue, or buy anything from Hot Topic."

Dr. C peers at me. "Color your hair blue?"

"I want to express myself," I tell her. "Someday I'm going to get a tattoo."

"For Pete's sake, nobody in this family is getting a tattoo!" shouts Dad. We all ignore him, except for Dr. C, who flinches and has to push her reading glasses back up her nose.

"I'm sorry," Mom says. "I can't allow you to express

yourself with blue hair and a backless dress at your brother's bar mitzvah."

Now the doc is chuckling. "Shopping is a nice bonding activity. Maybe you two can come to a compromise at the mall."

Dad makes a snorting noise. "Why don't you two go to Walmart and bond? Why does it have to be the mall?"

I'm not holding my breath for any great shopping and bonding with Mom. Unless Dr. C comes with us.

36

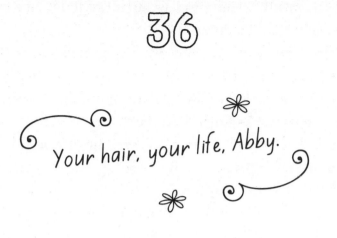

Your hair, your life, Abby.

Tony tells us *A Midsummer Night's Dream* is based on this one night of summer from Shakespearean times, when grown-ups and kids stayed up all night partying. He thinks we should celebrate summer's end and have our own version by hanging out in our classroom all night for a class sleepover.

"I can't go," Trina says at our picnic table. "I have an art festival in Key West with my parents that weekend."

"We're going to Disney," Amy says. "I can't go either."

"I'm going," I say. "What about you, Max?"

"Huh, what?" His mind is far away today. It's not like him. "Oh, I'm going."

Trina takes out a container of grapes from her backpack, pops a few in her mouth, and offers us some. We all take a few. "Do you guys think a nose piercing would look good on me?"

"You're allowed?" I ask. A shaved head would look good on her. Trina is really beautiful when you see past her clothing choices.

"I told you, my parents don't get involved in what I do," she says, rolling a grape around in her mouth.

"My parents won't even let me put a blue stripe in my hair for my brother's bar mitzvah," I say. "They think it's inappropriate. Everything is inappropriate with them."

"Your hair, your life, Abby," Trina says. "I recently told my mom I've become a fruitarian. No veggies, just fruit."

Amy and I laugh and shoot *she's so weird* looks at Trina.

I love our group.

I toss up a few grapes and attempt to catch them in my mouth. Some go in, some roll onto the grass. "Trina, is it true you invented an app for Microsoft? That's what I heard."

Trina lets out a long sigh. "Last year, I took apart Mrs. Carter's cell phone and fixed it. Then I took apart some of the school computers and fixed them. That's how that rumor got started, but it's not true. The school still uses me to fix computers in the lab sometimes. Technology and art are really easy for me. I don't like technology, though. Anybody have a pencil? I didn't do my homework."

"Amazing," Amy murmurs, shaking her head at Trina.

Trina *is* amazing. Here I am, trying to change for the better, do my work, control my mouth, and on and on. Trina is fine with being scattered. She doesn't struggle with who she is or have plans to turn over a new leaf. It must be nice to be happy with who you are.

Max hands Trina a pencil. "Listen, you guys, I've got something I need to tell you." He looks down at the ground instead of at us. After a few seconds, he lifts his head. "I'm moving back to Pennsylvania."

"What?" I didn't hear him right. I can't have.

"I'm going to live with my mother." I did hear him right. He's serious. And *happy* about it. His eyes are lighting up as he talks about his mother, who ditched him for another family. He says he'll be back to visit his dad a few times a year, so he'll be able to see us when he comes down to Florida.

All I hear in my head is *nonononononono.*

"You're moving?" I ask. "Like, definitely?"

"It's definite, yeah."

I see trees falling, skyscrapers imploding, cars crashing into walls.

"I leave in two weeks," he adds.

I search for words. "But you can't leave now. We just got our magic show together, and I'm working on something for us. . . . No. NO! You can't leave, Max. We need you here. All of us."

"Yeah," Trina says. "We have a good thing going. If you leave, it'll change our whole energy."

"Totally," says Amy. "You can't move."

"I have to," he says.

Suddenly, anger courses through my veins like a flash flood. "WHY?" I yell, throwing a cluster of grapes at Max. He puts his hands out. I pelt him, one grape at a time. "Why? Why? Why? You don't *have* to. You *want* to, even after she—"

"Abby, *stop!*" he shouts.

I stop. I'm panting, I'm so angry.

"Yes, I *want* to. Everyone deserves another chance. You said it yourself."

"I never said that!"

"Yes, you did! That day I found Simon. You said, 'Haven't you ever given someone another chance even if they've done something to hurt you? Caitlin hurts my feelings all the time, but I don't throw her away.' You said that."

I remember.

"I *have* to go," he says. "She's my mom. Don't any of you get that?" Max pulls a grape out of his shirt, gets up, grabs his laptop, and tucks it under his arm. We don't answer. "No, why would you? You all have these normal moms who bring you strawberries and let you paint on walls and take you to Disney. Well, I don't, okay?" His voice cracks like he's going to cry. "I have a mom who left me, but now she wants me back, and I have to give her another chance. She's my mom, and I have to go."

And with that, Magic Max walks away, leaving my eyes blurry with tears.

37

*I knew you'd be upset,
but I didn't expect to
be shot at with grapes.*

✳

Our test tomorrow is on all of *A Midsummer Night's Dream,* the biggest we've had so far, but it doesn't matter to me right now.

With my heart pounding, I call Max. "I'm so sorry," I say as soon as he answers.

"I knew you'd be upset, but I didn't expect to be shot at with grapes."

I laugh a little, relieved. He's not yelling at me. "It's a good thing I wasn't eating walnuts. You'd be black-and-blue."

"No, I'd just be blue, because you'd have killed me. I'm allergic."

"That would have been worse."

"Yeah." He chuckles. "Trina and Amy have been texting me, saying they're sorry I'm moving. They understand, though."

"I didn't understand at first, but I do now. I'm just sad you're going." My throat gets tight. *Don't cry, Abby. You'll make him feel worse.* "That's all."

"I wish my mom lived here."

"Me too. And I wish I hadn't reacted the way I did. I've been pretty good lately, but your news took me by surprise."

"No kidding. There's still a grape in my hair some-where."

We don't say anything for a little bit, just listen to each other breathe. Finally, Max goes, "We'd better get off the phone and study."

"I don't think I can. It'll be too hard to concentrate. You should have told us after the test."

He laughs. "Did you know that Shakespeare wore a hoop earring and invented the word *eyeball*?"

"I'm going to miss you, Max."

✳

I got a seventy-eight.

"What happened?" Tony asks me.

"I didn't study."

"Why not?"

Because all I could think about was Max moving. I shrug.

"Your essay section was disappointing," he says. "You left out a lot of supporting details. You could have taken more time."

"I know." According to my IEP, I'm allowed extra time on big tests, but so far, I've only used that option for national standardized tests.

Tony drums his fingers on his desk. "I've noticed your quad's study guides are exactly the same, word for word."

I swallow nervously. "We study together. That's why."

"Really?" Tony asks.

Don't lie, Abby.

"Okay, we're copying from Amy," I admit. "She takes the best notes, and to tell you the truth—"

"I wish you would."

"All that writing is a lot for me sometimes, even when I use a computer."

"Why don't you voice record your notes?" he asks. "You can email me an audio file, even for your study guide."

"You'll accept that?" I ask, surprised.

"Sure. There's more than one way to learn. Whatever works for you—"

"That definitely works for me. Talking is my thing!"

Tony's laugh is big and deep. "Talking is *definitely*

226

your thing. You'll probably be in my class in the fall, so tell me when you're having a problem. You're too smart to get a C. Okay?"

It's more than okay. "I might be in your class in the fall? Amazing!" Tony is the best teacher I've ever had.

"I think so too."

※

I'm still bummed about my test grade. I should have done better. "Why do the essays have to be worth so much?" I complain to Max after school at car pool. "In fact, why do I have to take English at all?"

"Because you might perform Shakespeare some-day, and you'll need to understand your lines." He hands me a red handkerchief. "Here, take this. You need it if you're going to cry over a test."

I grab it, and all these connected handkerchiefs come out of his sleeve. I pull and pull and pull, until finally the whole long string of handkerchiefs comes out. I throw them around my neck like a scarf. "It's your fault," I tell him. "All I can think about is you leaving, and I can't study." I worked on my video project for him instead. I'm almost done.

"Most famous people were terrible students, you know," he says. "Like ninety-two percent, I think."

"Are you making that up to make me feel better?"

"Maybe. Are you going to keep doing magic shows

after I leave? You could be more than an assistant. You can learn everything so we can double headline in Vegas someday."

"No," I say. "It's the two of us together that makes it work. Like Penn and Teller." We're quiet for a few minutes. I usually hate quiet, but it doesn't bother me when I'm with Max.

"It's nice when you're like this," he says. "You don't have to act all funny every minute, entertaining everyone around you. You can just be you, you know."

That's what a real friend is, I realize. Someone who likes you for just being you.

38

Our family is more of an onion than most.

Mom and I are at the mall shopping for my bar mitzvah dress. "Why are you so down?" she asks. "Is it because your teacher Terry called? He says you can raise that last grade, so don't let it upset you."

"It's Tony, not Terry, and that's not why I'm down. It's because my friend Max is moving away."

Mom puts her arm around me. "That's too bad. He seems like a nice boy. Maybe a pretty dress will cheer you up." As if it's that simple. We stop in front of a maternity store, because I want to take a picture of a dress in the store window. I text it to Beth with the message This would look good on U! She texts me back emoticons of smiley faces.

At Macy's, Mom pulls out five different dresses. Not one is the shade of blue I like, and they all look babyish. "Let's try Bloomie's," Mom says, so we head to Bloomingdale's. I don't like any there either.

"You know, summer school turned out to be the best thing for you," Mom says as we walk through the mall. "Your study habits are better, you're learning, you have new friends who are nice. Oh, did you see that Helpful Hints list I put on your desk?"

"Yes." I also saw the poster she put above my desk: IS WHAT YOU'RE DOING TODAY HELPING YOU ACHIEVE YOUR GOALS FOR TOMORROW? I wrote *NO* on it with a Sharpie because drama camp would have brought me way closer to achieving my goals for tomorrow. Although maybe not, according to Trina's meteor vs. star theory.

But Mom is sort of right, if I'm being honest. Had I gone to Star Lake, I wouldn't have discovered my knack for improv comedy or how fun it is to do magic shows with Max. I wouldn't have made friends with Trina, Max, or Amy.

Amy! Her parents' store is in the mall. Maybe I can convince Mom to spring for a designer dress. "Mom, have you noticed I've been cleaning my room more? And I put away the groceries yesterday without you asking me."

"Yes, Dad and I do see a big improvement in you."

"I haven't forgotten to take my pill once this summer. I've been working hard at school, and my behavior is better too."

"All that is true." *Say it. Say you're proud of me.* What she says is, "Someday you might take a page from Mike's book and be a real go-getter."

I stop in my tracks. Mom stops too. We weren't talking about Mike. We were talking about me. "Right." Angry lava churns in my stomach. *Respond, don't react.* People passing us throw curious looks our way. "Because Mike is an *angel.*"

"I didn't say he was an angel."

"You don't have to. It's obvious what you think. Drew's a geek, I'm The Great Disappointment, but hey, at least you have Mike." How could I ever have thought she'd say she was proud of me? "Let's go home. I don't want to shop anymore."

"Abby, wait." Mom puts her arm around my shoulders again. "Don't start with this. That's not what this day is supposed to be about. I want us to communicate."

I lift her arm off me. "Why do you have to compare me to Mike? We're TOTALLY different. Mike is a butthead. And he doesn't even know he's a butthead, which makes him more of a butthead. He is Nick Bottom from *A Midsummer Night's Dream!*"

So much for not reacting.

"I will not have you talk about your brother that way."

"Too late. I talk about him that way all the time. So does Drew."

Mom's words are measured. "Let's both stop. Take a moment, like Dr. C recommends. Want to go to California Pizza Kitchen? It's right there."

"Okay."

We go inside, get seated, and order. "I got a really nice call from Millennium Lakes about you," Mom says. "Did you call this man's children from Bonnie's office to try and get them to come and visit?"

"I did. Simon. That's the old man I visit when I go there. I don't understand why his kids don't visit. He's hilarious, and he's teaching me to play poker. I spoke to his daughter. She said she would come."

"She did, and brought her children. That was a thoughtful thing you did, Abby."

"What kind of kids don't visit their dad? Family is . . . family."

"You're right. Speaking of, do you remember seeing pictures of Mike's bar mitzvah?" Mom asks, although I don't think this is what we were "speaking of."

"Could we not talk about bar mitzvah stuff for one day, for the sake of Holy Moses and Abraham and everything in between?" I ask, picking up my phone to play a game.

Mom takes the phone out of my hand and places it

on the table facedown. "No phone. I'm talking to you. Do you remember?"

"Not really," I say.

"We had the party in the common room of our townhouse development. There were balloons, fold-out chairs, and sandwiches."

The waitress brings our waters. I take a sip. "And I care about this why?"

"Just listen. You know how I'm trying to understand you better?"

"Yeah."

"Well, I need you to try and understand Mike better. Did you ever stop to think how he must feel knowing about the big bash we're throwing for Drew? Or the affair we'll be throwing for your bat mitzvah next year?"

"What does that have to do with anything?"

"Abby, think about it. He had a small, modest party. Dad and I had student loans and all kinds of debt. We couldn't do for Mike what we do now for you and Drew. Mike knew Dad and I couldn't pay for sleepaway camp and expensive video cameras back then. That's why Mike worked so hard in high school for college scholarships and his own spending money." She waits a second to let all this sink in. "So I'm sorry if I *disagree* with you that he's a . . . whatchamacallit."

"A butthead. I didn't know any of this."

"Well, it's time you found out." She sips her water. "What do you think it does to him, seeing how much you and Drew have? I'm sure he can't help but compare."

Maybe that's why Mike and Beth are so interested in the big luxury homes they sell, country-club memberships, nice clothes, and fancy cars. They couldn't have it when they were kids, so it's important to them now. Maybe they dreamt about it the way I dream of an acting career.

I know from Meryl Streep movies that everyone in a family has a story, and all families have layers, like an onion. Our family is more of an onion than most.

"He does love you and Drew, you know," Mom says. "He just doesn't know how to show it."

I want to say, *He still acts like a jerk around me and Drew, like he did at Casa Lupita, and I don't know what Beth sees in him, and I'm sorry, but I still don't like him too much, even though he's my brother.* All that almost comes out. But I hit the pause button. "I'll try to keep what you told me in mind."

"That's all I ask."

Progress.

The waitress brings our food, pizza for me and salad for Mom. We eat for a few minutes. Then, out of the blue, Mom asks me something. "Why did you do it, Abby? The prank. Why did you leave the house without telling us? And then go mark up that car? We didn't bring you up that way. Was it Caitlin's idea?"

I put my pizza slice down. "Caitlin told me to get revenge. She said she knew where he lived. But it was mostly my idea. I felt like I had nothing to lose after flunking and missing camp." I drink my water. "I don't know. Maybe I wanted Mr. Finsecker to feel as bad as I felt."

Mom sighs. "All that time you were struggling in his class, and you never once came to us for help. Dad and I are not the enemy. We love you, and we want you to be happy."

"It didn't seem like it then, Mom. Like the night it happened, you didn't come in my room until you heard me making a mess, not even when I was yelling bad words and crying."

"You had to get your emotions out. We left you alone to vent."

"You should have come in anyway. You're my parents."

The waitress is eyeing us from the corner. We must be louder than we realize.

Mom cocks her head to one side. "You're tough, Abby."

"I'm like you."

She looks at me like I'm a fish in a tank. "No. You have a mind of your own. You're not *exactly* like me."

"I'm not exactly like anybody."

Mom throws her head back and laughs. It breaks the tension. "That's true! You are one of a kind." A good feeling comes over me when she says that.

We finish our meals, and Mom asks for the check. "You get mad as fast as I do," I tell her. "Maybe you could work on not being so stressed."

She nods, considering it. "I'll do that." She sips her drink. "Do you want to talk about anything else? Boys?"

"Ew, with you?"

"No, Abby, Oprah called. She wants to talk to you about your love life."

"Mom!"

"What?"

I smile at her. "You made a joke. You should do that more often."

She wrinkles up her nose. "You're right. I should."

"And, Mom?"

"Yes."

"This is nice."

Her eyes soften.

"Thanks for listening . . . for finding Dr. C. For everything. I'll always blame Mr. Finsecker for some of what happened, but I know why you didn't send me to camp. Anyway, thanks."

Mom's eyes tear up, and her hand flies to her

throat, clutching her necklace. And she says *I'm* dramatic.

"Oh, and, Mom?"

"Yes?"

"I think I know where I can get a dress for the bar mitzvah."

39

❋

I literally have to plan my funeral, because you're killing me.

❋

Teen Princess is a quick walk from California Pizza Kitchen. Amy is sitting behind the cash register reading a *Teen Vogue.* As soon as she sees me, she rushes out and hugs me.

"Hello again," Mom says to her. "Amy, right?"

"Yes, hi," she answers.

A beautiful, older version of Amy comes gliding out of a back room in a flowing maxi dress. "I'm Monique," she says. Mom holds out her hand. Monique takes it in both of hers. "I can't *tell* you how happy I am our daughters met. It's *lovely* to meet you both."

"I'm Rachel, this is Abby, and it's a pleasure to meet you too," Mom says warmly. "I feel the same way."

They start chatting. Amy leads me toward the back of the store. "So this is what you do on weekends?" I ask her.

Amy nods and says, "Can I help you?" We giggle.

"I need a fancy dress for my brother's bar mitzvah, but PS, my mom won't pay big bucks."

Amy leads me to racks in the way, way back and pulls out a minidress in my favorite shade of blue. It has a full, patterned skirt. "This is a Stella McCartney."

The dress fits like it was made for me. I twirl around, enjoying the way it flares out. I wish Max could see me in this. It would be great if we ever did a fancy magic show. "If I don't get this dress, I'll die. How much is it?"

"It's not from this season, so it's marked down."

I look at the price tag. "That much?" Amy nods. My heart is now somewhere at the bottom of the ocean. "No way is Mom going to pay that," I say sadly.

"Wait," Amy says. She comes back with black sequined sandals, long sparkly earrings, and a black headband. I put everything on.

My heart sinks even more as I admire myself. "I literally have to plan my funeral, because you're *killing* me." I twirl around and moan, "Why does it have to be so expensive? I don't want to take it off."

"Then don't. Stay here." She leaves and comes back with Mom. I hold my breath, wondering what she'll say.

Mom takes one look at me and gasps. "Oh, Abby. You *have* to wear this."

"It's not too expensive?"

She squints at the price tag, holding it at arm's length because she won't wear reading glasses. "We'll make it work. Let's get it." I squeal, jump up and down, hug Mom, throw my arms around Amy, and then do a little dance.

"You're a very talented stylist, young lady," Mom says to Amy, who looks about to burst with happiness. "I'll go and tell your mother we'll take everything."

Mom leaves, and Amy unzips the back of my dress. "I can't believe you called yourself nothing," I tell her reflection in the mirror. "Do you have any *idea* how talented you are?" I raise my arms up in a pose. "Look at what you created."

She copies my pose with her arms stretched up. Except I surprise her and tickle her under her arms. She jumps away, laughing, and then asks timidly, "Will you let me style you when you're on the red carpet?"

"Of course. That way we can meet all the celebrities together."

I twirl one last time before slipping off the dress. Amy is still smiling. So am I. This has been a really, really, really good day.

40

*What if one crawls
inside my mouth?*

It's the class sleepover. I've just walked in. About half of our class is already here. Max is sitting on a table with Kelvin, showing him a card trick. "I bent the corner of your ace," Max tells him. "You didn't notice because I was talking to you. That's called misdirection."

Max looks different tonight. It takes me a second to figure it out: white T-shirt, navy hoodie, dark jeans. New clothes. He looks sort of . . . cute. No kidding.

I'm *really* wishing he wasn't moving right now.

Before I have a chance to go over and say hi, Sofia whacks Kelvin with her pillow and yells, *"PELEA!"*

Apparently, this is the Guatemalan battle cry for a pillow fight. The ponytail girls go bananas hitting each other with their pillows and screaming in Spanish. I grab my pillow and jump in. So does Max. I get him good. He hammers me back. I'm about to retaliate when I hear "FREEZE!"

It's Tony, in jeans and a polo shirt, no tie, and khakis. He doesn't look like a teacher. He looks like one of us. Mrs. Shoop is right behind him in her usual cardigan. "Everyone needs to calm down, m'kay?" She tries to smile. It doesn't look like it comes easily to her.

"Penalties for unnecessary roughness!" Tony shouts. He tells us to listen up, reminds us about what the midsummer-night custom was all about in the olden days, and then has us push the tables against the wall, stack the chairs, and roll out our sleeping bags.

Pizza arrives next, and we sit around eating while Tony tells us disgusting facts about the Elizabethan age, like the boils people got with bubonic plague, and how people didn't brush their teeth, lived with rats, and only bathed a few times *a year*. Basically, they were like zombies from *The Walking Dead*.

The factoid that grosses us out the most is the love apple. An Elizabethan woman would cut an apple in half, rub it in her armpit, and then give it to her boyfriend or husband before he went away on a trip so he could smell her BO while he was away. BO was considered attractive. Everybody pretend barfs and goes "ew!"

"Oh, my," Mrs. Shoop says, adjusting her cardigan.

"I have something for you," Max says to me when Tony is done talking. "I wanted to give it to you before I leave."

"If it's a love apple, no thanks," I say, chewing on my pizza.

He wipes his hands on a napkin, reaches into his overnight bag, and pulls out a book titled *A How-To Guide to Stand-Up Comedy*.

I laugh. "I guess I need this."

"You don't. But I thought you'd like it."

"I have something for you. But not here."

"So you told me. But you don't have to give me anything. You already gave me you."

My pulse instantly speeds up. *Does he like me the way Trina thinks he likes me?*

"As an assistant, I mean," he adds.

"Oh. Right." My pulse goes back to normal.

After we eat, Tony tries to teach us these awkward, cuckoo Elizabethan dances, and afterward it's free time. Max and I look at videos of magicians on his laptop. At around ten, Tony waits until Mrs. Shoop leaves to go to the ladies' room, then surprises us with cans of silly string. Even Tony gets into it, spraying everyone.

Mrs. Shoop isn't thrilled when she walks back into the room and there's silly string everywhere, but we clean it up. After that we're all pretty tired, so we crawl inside our sleeping bags while Tony turns off the lights and shows us the movie *10 Things I Hate About You,* a modern version of Shakespeare's *The Taming of the Shrew.* Tony sits on the desk near where Mrs. Shoop is sitting in a chair. After a while I get up and ask him if I can go use the restroom.

"Sure," he says.

I turn to leave, then stop. "You're a great teacher, Tony," I tell him.

He tilts his head to one side, as if getting a good look at me. "Well, thank you, Abby. That's good to know."

"I'm surprised you didn't know it already." He smiles, then glances at Mrs. Shoop, who is obviously eavesdropping. I expected Tony to become the enemy. But I've learned more from him than any English teacher I've ever had, and it doesn't hurt that I can tell he likes me. That makes all the difference.

When I get back from the bathroom, Tony is in his sleeping bag. Mrs. Shoop is still in her chair, but she has a blanket over her. It's SO BIZARRE to be sleeping in the same room as teachers. I slink back into my sleeping bag. When the movie ends, I hear the slow, heavy breathing of a room full of people passed out.

"They're all asleep," Max whispers to me.

"Yeah."

"Are you cold?" I guess he can see I'm shivering. My T-shirt is really thin, and the air-conditioning is too strong in here. "Do you want my sweatshirt?"

"Are you sure you don't need it?" I ask. "*You'll* be cold." He doesn't answer, just takes it off and hands it to me. It's got that just-purchased-from-the-store-and-hasn't-been-washed-yet smell.

"So . . . uh, g'night," he says.

"G'night," I say back. His eyes are closed. Why haven't I ever noticed how long his lashes are?

This is weird. Max and I going to sleep right next to each other.

I hear a scratchy sound.

Palmetto bugs?

PALMETTO BUGS.

Palmetto bugs are not just any old bug. They are flying cockroaches so big they have faces. What if one crawls on me? What if one crawls inside my sleeping bag? *What if one crawls inside my mouth?*

There it is again. That noise.

"Max?" I whisper. "Are you sleeping?"

"Yes."

"Do you hear anything?"

"Yeah, you, unfortunately," he mumbles. "Stop wiggling your foot. It's making your sleeping bag crackle."

"Not that. Another sound." He doesn't answer. "Do you think there are palmetto bugs in here?"

"There might be. We're in Florida. Termites, ants, spiders, all sorts of bugs. They'll probably get inside your sleeping bag."

"Stop it."

He sighs. "Abby, don't be a canker blossom."

"A what?"

"Hermia calls Lysander that in the play," he says in a sleepy voice. "Now go to sleep."

"I can't. I'm scared." I can hear him laughing under his breath. "Stop laughing. I didn't tell you this before, but I have a major phobia about bugs. They really freak me out, especially when—"

The next thing I know, he's holding my hand. Just as a friend, because I'm scared, not because there is ANYTHING between us. Because there isn't. "Let's talk," he says. "You start."

"How did you flunk Finsecker's class? You're so smart."

"I was angry at my mom for leaving, angry at my dad for moving me out here, angry at you guys because I didn't know you and I didn't want to, angry at Finsecker because it was obvious he hated kids, just angry in general."

"So lemme ask you a question," I say.

"What?"

"By any chance, were you angry?"

He laughs. "So I blew off school, for the most part. I managed to pull it together at the end of the year in most of my classes. Just not Finsecker's."

"I'm glad you told me," I say.

We talk about new ideas for our act for when Max visits from Pennsylvania, plans for our website, his dad who never talks, which Nickelodeon shows we still secretly watch, which Will Ferrell movie is our favorite, his mom's new apartment, what he's packing, and what he's leaving behind. When I ask him if there's any way to change his mind about moving, he doesn't answer me, just takes deep, slow breaths. He's out. My eyelids get heavy. I drift off to sleep, my hand still in his.

When we wake up in the morning, we're still holding hands. Nobody sees, which is good. They might get the wrong idea.

41

*I have a choice.
I always did.*

It's the last week of summer school. Since the sleepover Max and I have been FaceTiming every night. We never run out of things to talk about. I talk to Trina too, but with Max leaving, I have to get in as much Max time as possible. My project just might convince him to stay. I'm going to give it to him tomorrow. I know I shouldn't get my hopes up, though.

I'm lying in bed, about to fall asleep, when my phone rings. I can't believe it. Caitlin. I guess she's calling because camp is ending soon.

"So did you get cast in *Legally Blonde*?" I ask her.

"I decided to work crew instead. I work the lights

or change the backdrops in between scenes. It's SO fun." Baloney. She didn't get a part. "How's your summer been going? Are you still hanging out with *Trina*?" She says *Trina* as if it means *lice*.

"Yeah, and Max and Amy. It's been the four of us this whole summer, basically."

"Well, I'm coming home next week, so you won't have to hang out with them anymore. And next year you can come to camp and have adventures, like me and Brett. You'll forget all about stupid dummy school."

"*Summer* school hasn't been as bad as I thought it would be."

"Come on," she laughs. "Be serious."

"I am. Max, Trina, and Amy made it fun. We've gotten really close."

She sighs, the way my mother does when she's running out of patience with me. "Abby, are you off your meds? When school starts—real school—you have to dump them."

"Why?"

"Because they're nothing like us!"

"You know what, Caitlin? I think you should seriously consider finding another best friend."

Did I just say that? Yes, I did.

"Don't be stupid. I'm your best friend."

"*Were* my best friend. Not anymore. You're not even my friend. You don't act like it, anyway." A mixture of anger and relief flows out of me as I say the words I've been thinking for so long. "And you can have Brett, for all I care. Good luck with that."

Silence. And then she asks, "I'm still going to your brother's bar mitzvah, right?"

"I don't know. I'm hanging up now."

I thought I needed Caitlin. She made me think I didn't have a choice, that I wouldn't ever be able to find another close friend, that she was my only friend option. But it's not true. I have a choice. I always did.

✳

I drop Mom's bottle of Sexy in my bathroom. Glass and perfume are everywhere. Drew holds his hand over his nose. "Why do you *always* break things and mess everything up?"

"Shut up and help me before Mom and Dad get home. Can you get me a towel?"

"Like your bedroom window and that man's car and your expensive pillow—"

"Stop!"

"You stop!"

Why is he mad? "Did I do something wrong?" Drew and I almost never fight. It's not like him to speak to me like this, although he has a few times this summer. "What did I do?"

He marches into my room, opens my closet, and

points to my new dress. "Mom was supposed to take me to get my suit for the bar mitzvah, but first your friends had to come over, and then she took you shopping instead. Now I don't have a suit, and there probably won't be time to alter it. My friends told me they needed to get theirs altered."

"How is it my fault that Mom forgot to get you your suit?"

"Do you have any idea how much time Mom and Dad spend dealing with you and all your stuff?"

"A lot, lately, I know, but—"

"Mom was so busy with you, she forgot about me. What else is new?"

"Calm down, Drew. She didn't forget—"

"Did you know Dad wanted you and me to have a double bar and bat mitzvah?"

"You mean a b'nai mitzvah?"

"Yeah. He wanted to do that to save money, since it would only be one party instead of two, but Mom said no, that I deserved one for myself without you stealing the spotlight, like you always do. Because you always, always do."

"I do not."

"You do too. We should have done one party anyway, because you're *still* taking up all their attention. I'll probably end up wearing sweatpants to my own bar mitzvah, thanks to you. But *you'll* have a new

252

dress." Drew stomps out, goes to his room, and locks the door.

I follow him and knock. He doesn't answer. I talk through his door. "Drew, the doctor told Mom and me to spend time together, I swear. That's why she took me shopping. If I'd known you needed your suit, I would have told her to take you instead of me." No answer from Drew. "Shouldn't Dad be taking you? Isn't suit shopping, like, a father-son thing?"

"Have you seen the way Dad dresses?" Drew answers through the door. Good point. Dad only wears team jerseys, baseball caps, and mismatched socks.

I knock again. Drew doesn't answer, so I use my secret weapon. "I'll tell Mom and Dad you played with airsoft guns when you went to Sameer's house last week." My parents don't allow any kind of toy gun, but they especially can't stand airsoft guns, because they look like real machine guns. Sameer has about twenty airsoft guns.

Drew opens his door. "How did you know that?"

"I saw the pellets stuck to the Velcro on your sneakers when you came back from his house."

"I can't believe you noticed that."

"Believe it. I notice everything." He looks irritated. But he's not mad anymore. Drew is like Dad. He gets ticked off for about thirty seconds and then he's back to normal. "Mom can take you tonight after dinner.

No one is going to steal your spotlight. Not even me. Your bar mitzvah is going to be great. *You're* going to be great."

He shrugs. "Maybe."

"Help me clean up the perfume mess?"

"Fine, but you have to teach me how to play poker like Simon taught you." I get a plastic bag, and Drew helps me pick up all the shards and wipe up the perfume with a towel. "I don't care if you steal my spotlight," he says. "I don't like being in it anyway."

"Then why did you get so mad at me?"

"Because as usual it's all about you, all the time. It gets old."

"I'm sorry."

After we clean up, we go to my room and sit on the floor. Drew shuffles and says, "Take out the jokers."

"Who says you can't use jokers in this game?"

He takes them out. "You can't use jokers for anything. Ever."

"So jokers are useless?" I say, more to myself than Drew.

"Yeah. Jokers are useless." He throws them across the room. They land in a pile of magazines by my bed.

"That's me, a useless joker," I mumble.

"Joker *cards* are useless. Jokers are important in real life. Everyone needs to laugh. Besides, you can drop your joker act when you want to."

"The thing is," I say, "I don't know if I truly am that joker, if it's an act, or if it's just become a habit."

"Maybe it's all three. There's a lot more to you than just jokes, you know."

The way he says that chokes me up, and my eyes get a little blurry, and the line I was about to blurt ("Yoda man, bar mitzvah boy") gets stuck in my throat.

It's time. I'm in front of my computer. Everything has been transferred and edited, thanks to Drew showing me how. I didn't start this as my good-bye to Max. It began as a way to promote our magic-show business, but now that he's leaving, our magic-show partnership is over.

I upload the three videos I have to YouTube.

Then text the link to Max, Trina, and Amy.

※

"HOW COULD YOU DO THIS TO ME?!" Max shouts into the phone.

I don't understand.

"Do what to you?" I ask. "Didn't you watch them? Didn't you see how funny it is?"

"Yes, I watched them! Take them down. Now. NOW. I can't believe you!"

"I was promoting our magic show, like marketing. You said you wanted humor. That's why you asked me to be a part of your act, right? This is *funny*." I remember a phrase I learned from a business reality show. "I was promoting our brand."

"Promoting our brand? Are you *crazy*?!" Max squeaks. "I'll never be able to get another magic gig again, thanks to you. You promised you would never embarrass me in public. You *promised*. And now you've humiliated me on a GLOBAL level. Take. It. Down."

"Okay, I'll take it down. I'm sorry."

His voice is dead flat. "I'm tired of hearing you're sorry. I'm glad I'm moving away from you. All you do is wreck everything."

All the air goes out of me. "Max, you don't mean that. Part of the reason I did this was because I thought you'd, I don't know—"

"You thought what?"

"That you might stay after you saw all the good times we had."

"*Stay?* You thought I'd want to STAY after you did this to me? Now I *have* to leave! You've made me look like the world's dumbest magician. I never should have asked you to help me. That was the worst decision I ever made."

I'm numb. It's like my insides have been run over by a car.

I watch the videos again. Max dropping metal rings everywhere, scrambling on the floor to pick them up, an old lady with a walker squeaking by while he's performing, audience members yawning, kids screaming and crying, carrots flying out at them, a mother running toward the camera screaming angrily, Max going "um . . . um . . . um . . ." into a microphone.

Over two hundred views already, and rising.

I thought it would be funny. I thought people would see it and think we were a good comedy team. Now I see what Max sees.

I've made him look like a nerd who doesn't know what he's doing.

This wasn't marketing. Or true comedy. I should have realized I was making Max look stupid at the one thing he takes pride in doing well, the one thing he takes seriously. Magic.

How could I have been so off the mark?

My phone dings with a text. It's Trina.

Y did u do it?

Another text, from Amy this time.

Amy: Saw Utube videos.
Max sez he is done w/u.
Make up w/him!

> **Trina:** Plz take them down.
> Im askin 4 Max

Amy: did u see the
comments?

I scroll down to the comments section. *Abracadorcus. What a dweeb! I'd want my money back. How old are these kids, twelve? That moron will never have a career in magic.*

I feel sick.

I did this. Me.

All you do is wreck everything.

My hands shake as I click on my mouse to take the videos off YouTube.

Now they all think I'm a horrible person. They hate me.

I thought TNTRML was my lowest point, the worst thing I ever did. I was wrong.

This is.

Amy and Trina come over. "I meant it as publicity for us," I say, trying not to cry. "You've got to believe me. I thought Max would laugh. I thought he'd *love* it."

"How?" Trina asks. "How did you think that?"

"I thought I was showing how funny we are, like reality comedy, the kind you see on *Impractical Jokers*."

"Except Max was the butt of every single joke," Trina says gently.

"Yeah," Amy whispers. "You showed him doing everything wrong."

"I was in it too. I made fun of myself."

"Not like you made fun of Max," Trina says, shaking her head. "People reposted it. It went viral."

"It was a mistake." I start crying. Badly. Ugly-faced, snot-nosed crying. Trina and Amy both hug me. "Do you h-h-hate m-me?" I ask between sobs.

"No," they both say.

"But you've got to fix things with Max," Trina says.

"I know. Any ideas?" I ask.

"I wish we could tell you," Trina says. "The answer will come to you."

There is no answer to how to fix this.

After they leave, I break down in new sobs. I lie on my bed and let it all out.

It dawns on me that I've lost my best friend. My

BFF is now Max. Not Caitlin. Trina and Amy run a close second place, but Max and I have a connection that is extra special.

Now I've probably lost him forever. He's moving, and he'll leave hating me.

I blew it.

43

He's done with me.
Forever.

It's been a day since YouTube-gate. Hundreds of people saw my videos. No word from Max. I've left him messages, tried to talk to him in school, wrote him an apology note. I also texted him:

Don't U think U shld give me
another chance? Ur giving ur
mom another chance.

He didn't text back. Max won't as much as glance

in my direction, and he won't sit anywhere near me. Tony let him pull up a chair at Kelvin's quad.

He's done with me. Forever.

Trina and Amy told me he's packing, and his Dad is driving him up next Saturday. They said the deal is that he's going to live with his mom for one year on a trial basis.

Will he call me to say good-bye?

✳

Family dinner at Little Italy tonight. It's Grandma's favorite restaurant. I like it too, but not for the food. The waiter Nick and I have a routine where we shout at each other and pretend to speak Italian, like this:

"Luciano Pavarotti arugula?" Nick asks.

"Lasagna Gianni Versace," I answer. I usually belt it out, but my heart isn't in it tonight.

Mom rubs her temple like she has a headache. My Italian routine with Nick drives her nutso. "Mozzarella biscotti pizzeria," I tell Nick, handing him the menu. Grandpa laughs his dentures off. Literally. He has to adjust them back in his mouth. Drew gets it all on camera.

Ding. A text from Amy:

Saw this online—it
might get ur mind off
everything w/Max—u
should do it.

I click on the link.

KID NIGHT AT THE COMEDY CAVE!

Are you a funny kid between the ages of 10 and 13? Then bring
your jokes, your family, and your friends to the Comedy Cave
Kids' Open Mic Night this Saturday at 7 p.m. and show us your
yuks. No experience necessary.

The last thing I am is a funny kid. I know that
now. It's clear I have no idea what is funny and what
is hurtful, and I shouldn't be anywhere near a comedy stage.

Still, I read it aloud to everybody. "Comedy clubs
are sleazy," Grandma says. "My friends and I would
never be caught dead in one. It's not for a nice girl
like you, Abby."

"Right," Mom agrees, fanning herself with a menu.
"You're too young for a nightclub environment. Besides, you're grounded again, don't forget." Mom
found out about my YouTube debacle. She feels bad
about Max leaving, but she says there have to be
consequences for me using the Internet irresponsi-
bly, especially when I wasn't supposed to be on social

media at all. I don't consider YouTube social media, but my parents do, and *no social media* was on my grounded list. So I'm back to no Netflix and an early bedtime. The way I'm going, I'll be grounded in some form for the rest of my life.

"Aw, let her try the comedy thing," says Grandpa. "She's a pistol. I've always said so."

"Why does she need to try it?" Grandma says. "Stay out of it, Solly."

Everyone weighs in. Only Drew and Grandpa think I should do it. The others don't think I should, and worse, they don't think I can. The more they talk, the more cheesed off I get. What do they know?

Sure, I bombed in front of my class, but that feels like a million years ago.

Maybe, just maybe, in spite of the horrible YouTube mistake, I could still be a funny kid.

Max told me it would be stupid to give up. My friends thought I had what it takes.

But performing stand-up in a real live comedy club is too frightening to consider. Just me, a microphone, and a spotlight? A silent audience or, worse, a mean audience?

Although maybe, just maybe, I'd have an audience laughing hysterically, applauding, the way they do for the comics I see on TV. Maybe that's the Abby show I should be working toward. A tingle runs through me as I picture it.

"Maybe you *should* try stand-up comedy, Abby," Dad says. "You can't be any worse than those ding dongs on the comedy channel." *Gee, thanks, Dad.*

"I appreciate your support," I say, my voice dripping with sarcasm.

"No comedy club," Mom says. "That's final."

I text Amy.

Thx for sending — can't do it

"Hey, if Abby wants to make a fool of herself, let her," says Mike.

"For your information, during Shakespeare's time comics were called fools," I tell Mike. "*Fool* wasn't an insult, it was a profession. So, thanks for the compliment."

"Well, nowadays a fool is a dummy," says Mike.

"You should know," I shoot back. Even with everything Mom told me, Mike gets on my last nerve.

"I think you're funny, Abby," Beth says, eating a garlic roll.

"Thanks, Beth," I say. "You look . . ." I was about to say "You look good rounder," but I stop myself. *Don't.* "You look good. Great."

Mouth, you don't own me anymore. She winks at me. I wink back.

"Right, Abby's funny," Mike says. "If you're a two-year-old."

266

"Stop it, Mike!" Mom says. "Stop putting Abby down all the time. Do you hear me? No more."

For once, Mike is speechless. Mom never talks to him like that.

"Mom is right," Dad says, looking at Mike. His voice is quiet, stern. "We should support each other in this family."

Mike starts to open his mouth with a comeback, but Mom's and Dad's expressions stop him.

I look at my parents gratefully. "I appreciate your support." This time, I mean it.

44

*Three words for them.
They. Are. Wrong.*

Dr. C has her blond-streaked hair in a bun today. "I've been in contact with your teacher, Tony. He says you've improved your calling out and impulsive behavior, so I'm very surprised about this YouTube business. You were doing so well. What happened? You want to tell me about that?"

I shake my head.

"You sure?" Mom asks. "That's why we're here. Your YouTube video cost you a friendship."

None of this is helping.

Dr. C waits. I don't know what to say. "I can see

you're upset with yourself," she says. "It's a hiccup, Abby. A setback, that's all."

"Losing Max is more than a hiccup." My voice wobbles, and my throat gets tight. "I made a major mistake, but it wasn't a, um . . ." I search for the word. ". . . an impulse. I thought my YouTube videos would be great. I thought they would be something that they weren't. I didn't see them the way other people did. I thought they were funny."

"So it was an error of judgment," Dr. C says, peering at me over her rhinestone glasses. "A poor decision."

That sounds right. "Yeah. But I don't want to talk about it. It makes me feel bad."

"You don't want to talk about Max?"

"No."

"Okay, let's talk about how you can move forward with good decisions, not bad ones. Tell me about the good decisions you've been making."

I shrug.

There's a fly buzzing in the corner of the window. I wonder if it will get out through the opening. It keeps circling around it, almost escaping but missing every time. That fly is like me. The opening is there, but I can never get through to where I want to be. The *bzzz* is faint, but I can hear it.

"Abby?" asks Dr. C. "What's been going well lately?"

"What? Oh. Going well. Fewer conversational accidents," I say. "I think I might be learning to use my filter. I'm getting better at stopping myself. But I still react big time when I get mad. Like when Max told me he was leaving, I threw grapes at him."

"You threw grapes at him," Dr. C repeats.

I start giggling. It's inappropriate but hard to stop, even with Dr. C's serious face aimed right at me. "We laughed about it later."

"You talk to Max a lot?" Dr. C asks.

That stops my giggling—the realization that I don't talk to him anymore. "Yeah, we talk on the phone and in class too, but I stopped doing that as much or Tony said he'd move my seat." I don't know if Max will ever talk to me again now.

Dr. C listens, typing on her laptop. "We're going to discuss managing your emotions, but first, I need to tell you that I used to get in trouble for talking too much, just like you."

"You did?" I ask, surprised.

"I did. Now I talk all day, and listen too, and I'm good at it. Your emotions run high because you're passionate. You *feel* things. That will make you a good actress someday. Your biggest flaw can be your greatest asset. Remember that."

"I will." I'll have no choice but to remember that. Because I know I'll never be able to change all my flaws. I'll just get better at managing some of them, maybe.

"I will too," Mom says. "That's a good one to re-member, Abbles."

✳

I'm playing a game on my phone when it rings. Why is Caitlin calling me? *Don't pick up.* It rings and rings. "Hello?" I'm too curious.

"I'm sorry about what I said, about dumping your new friends."

I don't answer her.

"Hello?"

"I'm here."

"So, are we still friends?"

"Honestly, I don't know."

"So you're friendship-breaking-up with me, just because you made new friends *without* me? *I'm* the one who should be mad at *you*. Don't you think you should give me another chance?"

That's exactly what I asked Max. Sometimes you run out of chances.

"We're not as close as we used to be because of the way you've treated me, not because of my new friends," I say. "Didn't *you* make new friends at camp?"

"Of course I made friends, you idiot."

"See? Friends don't call each other idiots." And then it hits me. It wasn't *me* who needed to worry about finding other friends, it was *Caitlin*. It's been Caitlin all along, making me think I needed her when really it was the other way around. She hasn't been in touch this summer because she didn't want me to know she wasn't making new friends at camp.

"So are you having any adventures?" she asks, assuming I'm taking her back.

"Actually, I *am* having an adventure," I say.

"Really?"

The lie comes out before I can stop it. "Yeah, I'm doing stand-up comedy at a comedy club this Saturday night. At the Comedy Cave."

"Stand-up comedy? You?"

"Yeah." I brace myself for the put-down.

"Wow, that's new for you."

"Yeah, but I can do it."

"If you say so. I thought you wanted to be an actress."

"Who says I can't do both?"

Caitlin doesn't say anything for a few seconds. Then she snorts. "Well, break a leg, I guess." *It's obvious she doesn't think I can do it.* "They'll yell *boo* and stuff if you're bad."

"I'm aware of that."

"I just want you to know what you're in for."

"Thanks." My voice is cold.

"Listen . . . I'm sorry about calling you an idiot. But did you ever think we're not as close as we used to be because you've had this whole other life on the soccer team, and in plays, and now summer school? What about me? I try out for everything and *never* make it. Even here, I didn't make it into one single production." I can't remember the last time Caitlin cried, but it sounds like she's about to. "You know where they put me? On the crew. Holding up backdrops or helping talent change in between scenes. That's what they call the actors. *Talent.* To remind the rest of us that we don't have any."

I can't think of anything to say, except, "Maybe next year you'll get a part. At least you got to go to camp."

"It wasn't how I thought it would be. I won't be coming back. You should go, though. You would have gotten a part." It's the first time she's said anything slightly nice to me in months.

I feel sorry for her after she's revealed all that, but why didn't she tell me sooner? A real friend would have, instead of treating me badly. "I gotta go," I say.

"Are we friends?" she asks.

No. Say no. "Maybe. But you have to be nice to my summer school friends, even after school starts. And to me. That's the deal."

"Okay," she says.

I guess I do want to give Caitlin another chance.

We talk for a few minutes before hanging up. She says she's my shoulder to cry on after the comedy show if I need it, so I should call her afterward.

How dare Caitlin automatically assume I'm going to fail? Haven't I been teaching myself stand-up skills working with Max? Sure, they're magic shows, but they count. Plus, I've been learning a lot from the comedy book Max gave me.

Max.

Mom told me I wasn't allowed to do the comedy show.

I have to move forward with good decisions.

But I also need to prove to myself, to everybody, that I have something special.

So what if Caitlin and my family don't believe in me?

I believe in me.

Three words for them. They. Are. Wrong.

I'll show Caitlin. I'll show everybody. This is a good decision.

I take out a notebook and jot down some of the rules of comedy I read in the book Max gave me.

1) *Make fun of yourself.*
2) *Make fun of your family, your life.*
3) *Be honest.*

4) *Be fearless.*

5) *Make fun of what gets you angry. Outrageous comedy comes out of <u>rage</u>.*

I look over the list.

And start writing my set.

45

❋

Mom, most teenagers don't choose a miniskirt based on whether it hides stretch marks. You're not fooling anybody.

❋

I walk out onto the stage and the first thing I realize is . . . I'm in the spotlight, where I belong. The second thing I realize is . . . I have to pee.

Really bad.

Reallyreallyreallyreallyreally bad.

But that's not the worst part. There's the fear. The sweat on my brow. My hammering heart. And the possibility that I'll never be as good as the kids who went on before me.

I have to pee so badly. Grandpa dropped me off here. He's the only person on the planet who knows I'm doing this. He was thrilled to hear I was giving it a try, but I made him promise to leave and swore him to secrecy. He told Mom and Dad I'm helping him with inventory at Pewter Palace. I didn't tell anyone at school about this either, so at least if I fail, my failure will be private.

My eyes are dry. I was so hyper focused on writing this material, I stayed up until two in the morning.

It's dark except for the votive candles on the tables. I wonder if they can see the blue chalk streak I put in my hair backstage. The streak makes me feel creative and hipster-cool. At least I look the part, even if I blow it.

I can barely see the audience. My index cards are on the stool next to me. The Comedy Cave gave us seven minutes each. My heartbeat is a machine gun, *bambambambambambambam.* Why can't I remember how my set starts? *One . . . two . . . three . . .*

Just be yourself. Do what you practiced.

This. Is. *THE ABBY SHOW.*

My eyes adjust to the darkness. I tug the hem of my black shirt, smooth it over my black jeans. I'm wearing all black, like the pros do. In the front row, I spot the boy who went on before me. He was nice backstage. Friendly. His eyes meet mine. *Go ahead,* they seem to be saying. *You'll be fine.*

I pace the stage like I've seen comedians do on Comedy Central, the way I pace when I'm on the phone. Pacing helps me stay focused. I look at my cards. Key words pop out: *Grandpa ATM machine* and *Mom on Weight Watchers.*

"Hi, I'm Abby," I start. "My grandpa drove me here. He supports my comedy career. Every time I see him, he gives me twenty bucks. He tells me I'm his favorite grandchild. He also tells my brother that." I hear some chuckles. "I don't let Grandpa know that we know what he's doing, because he's my only source of income." A few laughs. "Grandpa is basically an ATM machine with dentures." I get a few chuckles here and there. Not the wall-shaking, knee-slapping hysteria I'd imagined, but I'm not tanking.

Yet.

"And then there's Grandma. You could be an axe murderer, but if you're Jewish, she'll love you. She'll invite you to dinner, give you Jell-O, tell you to hang your axe in the closet, and since you're up, please make the air colder." More people laugh. "Then there's my mother. She tries to dress like a teenager, and I'm like, 'Mom, most teenagers don't choose a miniskirt based on whether it hides stretch marks. You're not fooling anybody.'" Lots of people laugh at that one. A few clap. "Actually, she has nicer clothes than I do and looks better in them. I dress like Little Orphan Abby. I might actually be an orphan. I'm nothing like my family.

"Everyone in my family has problems. My dad recently went bald, and not in the cool way. He used to have a great head of hair, but now it's all moved to his back and chest. My dad's chest is so hairy, I saw crop circles on the front of him the other day, but then I realized it was just his nipples." Huge laugh. Yes! "Watch for my dad's back on SyFy." Lots of laughing now.

"I have my own problems too. Plenty of problems. I'm grounded, and I so don't deserve to be." *Wait a beat.* "All because I blew off this one class." *Wait.* "Oh, and I lied about my grades." *Wait.* "Oh, let's see, what else, oh, yeah, I snuck out of my house, vandalized a car, and got busted. I also broke a window. And misplaced an elderly person while I was volunteering. Oh, um, and then there was this YouTube scandal that went viral? But that's all. What's the big deal?"

The whole room cracks up. "I wasn't the best student last year. I believe the official term for my academic level is Lost in Space." The laughs keep coming. "I guess it's because I have ADHD, Attention Deficit/ Hyperactivity Disorder. The problem is that I get, like, easily distracted." *Wait. Eyes up. Eyes down. Stare at the lights. Tap lip with finger.* "Um . . . what was I just talking about?" The whole room explodes in laughter. It's a beautiful sound. A heat spreads through me, warming my insides. "I'm also diagnosed as gifted. *Twice exceptional,* it's called. My mother read that Bill Gates is twice exceptional." *Scratch your head again. Get that blank look on your face.* "Yeah,

I tell her not to count on me buying her a dream house and a Mercedes with my genius money." More laughs. "I might be able to get her a plastic shed and a go-cart. Used."

"My brother is having a big BM." I wait. "Bar mitzvah." The laughs come. "Supposedly, this makes him a man. Yup, a thirteen-year-old man, ladies and gentlemen. If that's true, he'll be the only man I know who still sleeps in pajamas with feet." I pause to let people finish cracking up. "I'm supposed to have a bat mitzvah next year, but I should probably have it, like, never, if it means growing up. I'm afraid of bugs, I break things, I'm forgetful, and I say things that are way out of bounds."

I keep going—I talk about how Grandma thinks Whoopi Goldberg is Jewish, the way my parents do the robot when they dance together. I imitate the way Grandpa blows his nose. I imitate my mother looking at her rear end in the mirror, squeezing in her butt cheeks to try and make her butt look smaller. I pretty much roast my entire family.

But mostly, I roast myself. I mime myself looking for things and spacing out in class. I do all my crazy characters, the ones I do in my room in front of my mirror. I interview myself. I show them the bruises on my legs and have audience members guess which countries they look like. I talk about how I apologize for something every single day, how my superhero name is The Apologizer and my superpower is the ability to tick someone off with a single word.

The crowd roars.

Eddie the MC is giving me the cutoff sign. Has it been seven minutes already? The whole front row is beaming up at me. "Thanks, you've been a great audience, and I wouldn't trade this night for anything," I say. "Okay, well, maybe I'd trade it for my own comedy special. HBO, are you listening?" I spot a lady in the audience wearing long, dangling earrings. "Or maybe those earrings you're wearing." I step off the stage, hold out my hand to her. She chuckles. I wiggle my fingers. "No, seriously. I need the earrings." She laughs, but doesn't budge. I wiggle my fingers some more. "I'll give them back. Promise. Hand over the earrings." The whole room is hysterical, clapping as she takes them off, puts them in my hand. I take off my own hoop earrings, hand them to her, say, "Let's trade," and put in her danglies. Then I jump up onto the stage and run off, saying, "Thanks! Gotta go!"

I did it.

I DID IT!!!!

I've finally done something right.

And then it comes. The sound I was waiting for. Like a floodgate opening, it rushes in. Clapping. Whistles, whoops. Going on and on. They love me.

Me!

46

I'm dead.

Backstage, I give the lady's earrings to Eddie the MC, who says, "Great job, kid." He goes out into the audience and hands them to the lady, who hands him my hoops, which he gives back to me. Tonight, I have proof that my mouth, the thing that always got me in trouble, the thing I thought was my enemy, might just be the best thing I have going for me. I can hold on to my dreams. *Your biggest flaw can be your greatest asset.*

Truth. Thanks, Dr. C.

I try to tone down my giant pleased-with-myself

smile, but I can't wipe it off my face as I walk through the door that leads into the lobby.

But when the door closes behind me and I look up, I stop smiling. Because there, in a row, waiting for me, is my entire family. Grandpa, Grandma, Mom, Dad, Drew, Mike, and Beth. All of them.

I'm dead.

They rush toward me, all talking at once. Grandpa gets to me first. "I had to tell them, I had to tell them," he says, throwing his arms around me in a hug.

Someone pats my back. It's Dad. "You were a real pro out there, buddy. A real pro."

"You were funny, you really were," echoes my mother, smiling big. *Smiling.*

Hang on. Hang on just a minute.

Did I hear her correctly? I untangle myself from Grandpa, scan Mom's face. "You're not mad?" I ask her, shocked. She doesn't answer, just shakes her head no. She bites her lower lip, sniffs. The look on her face. It isn't anger, it's . . .

"I'm so proud of you," she says. "So very proud."

Pride. And then she says it again. "I am so incredibly proud of you, Abby."

I can't help crying a little. I'm not The Great Disappointment. Not tonight. Maybe I never was.

She hugs me and keeps hold of me, swaying a little

bit, and that chokes me up even more, because I can't remember the last time I hugged my mother tightly for a long time. My blue hair chalk gets all over her shirt, and she doesn't even care.

I pull back from her arms so I can see her face again. "But you said stand-up comedy is sleazy. You didn't want me to do this."

"So? A person can change her mind, can't she? You changed my mind." She's crying a little too. Maybe she never will approve of everything I wear or all the jokes I make, but she's accepting me, letting me be me.

"But I made fun of you," I say, searching the faces of Dad, Drew, Grandma, Grandpa, Mike, and Beth. "I made fun of all of you."

"Yeah, you did," Mike says, not sounding happy about it.

"Give us a little credit, Abby," Dad says.

"Right, we know it's a performance and it's all for the act," says Mom. "Okay, well, mentioning my stretch marks . . . maybe that one went a little too far. But I understand you have to get your material from somewhere. All comedians insult their families, right, Howard?"

Dad nods, agreeing. "And you insulted yourself more. That's the mark of a true comic." My parents are suddenly experts on comedy?

"Let's face it!" Grandpa shouts. "We're hilarious!" He points at me. "I always said my Abby was going places. You're on your way, kiddo!" For a second Grandpa makes me think of Simon. He would have loved this. Maybe I'll talk to Bonnie about doing a comedy show for Millennium Lakes.

That makes me think of Max.

Drew, who is filming all this, still hasn't said anything. "You're not mad at me either?" I ask him.

He shrugs. "I don't sleep in those pajamas anymore."

"I know," I say. "I made that one up."

"It's okay."

"I'm going to tell all my friends that my granddaughter is a regular Joan Rivers, may she rest in peace," announces Grandma.

"But what about how your friends wouldn't be caught dead at a comedy club because they're so sleazy?" I ask her.

"This one's not so bad," she says.

Mom and Grandma will never admit they were wrong. But who cares? I can*not* believe their reaction. This is amazing. I roasted them, mocked them like crazy, and not only are they not mad, they're *happy* about it. How did this happen?

I finally feel like they see me for who I am, like they get me.

"You did great, Abby," Beth says. "You were funny." She hugs me and puts my hand on her belly. I feel something.

"Was that a kick?" I ask, excited.

"Nah, just indigestion," she says. She touches my blue streak. "I like that. Very you."

Mike puts his hand on my shoulder. "Listen, we better get going." He gives me a stiff hug. "You were funny. Funny-*looking*. Ha-yah!" He karate chops the air. "Now who's the comedian? See you on late-night TV someday, huh?" He and Beth kiss me and leave. I guess Mike means well. He just doesn't know how to show it. I know what that feels like.

"I still say Whoopi Goldberg is Jewish," Grandma says, and we all laugh.

"Does this mean I'm not grounded anymore?" I plead with Mom and Dad. "Please. Pleaseplease pleaseplease*pul-leeeeeeez*."

"You lied to us to come out here tonight," says Mom. "You knew you were still supposed to be grounded, and you broke the rules."

"But I've learned my lesson," I whine. "After every-thing that's happened this summer, don't you think I've been grounded long enough? Can we just get rid of the list already?"

"Okay," Mom says.

And just like that, I'm not grounded anymore.

Drew smiles at me. I thank Mom and Dad about a hundred times.

"Do you want to go out and celebrate with your friends tonight?" Dad asks.

"They don't even know I'm here. I told them I wasn't doing this."

"What are you talking about?" Grandpa says. "They were sitting in the back row with us."

Just as I'm about to insist he must be mistaken, the double doors open and people stream into the lobby. Leading the pack is Amy, Trina, and Max.

MAX!!!!

Behind them are Tony and other kids from class—Kelvin, Graham, and Sofia and her Guatemalan crew. They come up to me woo-hooing and shouting, "Surprise!" "Incredible!" "You were great!" "Hysterical!" and "Totally!"

"You've got skills, girl!" Kelvin says with a big smile.

"Yeah! Seriously. My stomach hurts from laughing."

"Yeah, me too," says Graham.

They all came to see me. I can't believe it. "Thanks, you guys." I hug all of them, even the ones I don't know well.

"What are you doing here?" I ask Max. "You said

288

I made you look like the world's dumbest magician, and I embarrassed you . . . but you're here."

He looks down at me with this sweet expression. "I forgive you. I know your idea of funny isn't always mine. It's okay. I'm over it now." I can't speak. I'm too choked up. He hugs me. I float away, whiffing the scent of lavender fabric softener from his shirt. He lets go first. "I know you did it to try and make me stay."

"Did it work?" I ask into his ear.

"No. I've got to go."

"You'll never know how sorry I am. You're my best friend, Max."

He nods. He doesn't have to say anything. I know he's saying I'm his best friend too.

I turn to the others, who are watching us like we're in a movie. "How did you guys know I would be performing here? I didn't tell anyone."

Max answers, "I had a feeling, so I called here and asked if you were in the lineup. Then I spread the news, and everyone wanted to come."

Kelvin, Sofia, and the other ponytail girls say some nice things to me, about how I was the best one up there and how my parents are so nice to let me use them for my comedy material (!!!!!). They leave after that, but Max, Trina, Amy, and Tony stay.

"I've got to go," Tony tells my parents, "but I just want to tell you what a talented kid you've got there.

She's a gem. I can't tell you how happy I am that she's in my class. Abby, you're a star!" Tony says with a wave. He heads out.

"What a difference from Mr. Finsecker," Mom says. "He's wonderful."

"He is," I say, feeling choked up again. "The best. It was his idea that I try stand-up in the first place."

Dad puts his arm around me. "Your friends seem like a nice bunch too. What do you say we celebrate next door at Baskin-Robbins?" Mom doesn't tell Dad how many points a cone of rocky road is, and she doesn't tell me I can't have sugar. "Would you kids like to join us for ice cream?" Dad asks everyone. "My treat."

"No, thanks," Trina says. "I don't do dairy. I'm a fruitarian. But I'll come to be social."

Grandma and Mom stare at Trina's pajama pants. "You're a what?" Grandma asks her.

"A fruitarian," Trina repeats.

Grandma looks at Mom. "A fruitarian. So she's not Jewish?" Mom shushes her.

Luckily, my parents and grandparents sit at a faraway table at Baskin-Robbins, giving me semi-privacy with my friends. I invite Drew to sit with us. He films us talking and laughing. Amy takes pictures of us to post online. We put our arms around each other, make faces, and hold up our ice creams.

I love my life.

We talk about how Tony's class is ending in a few days. Looking back, I remember when I thought summer school was the end of the world. It turned out to be the best, most fun summer I ever had. And I learned a lot, about myself and about English.

Tony already told me I'm getting a B+ for my final class grade, not too bad. Trina says he took us to the next level spiritually and intellectually, and it was a communal learning experience.

Max and Amy go over all the parts of my set that had them cracking up. "I can't believe your mom was laughing," Max says. "Laughing!"

"I can't believe it either," I say. I look around the table at my summer friends. On the first day of school, I told Caitlin they were all wackos, and let her make mean jokes about them. I've never been more wrong.

Trina is fun and unique, even a genius, apparently. She's been there for me this summer, been there for all of us. She always knows the right thing to say to make a person feel better. She's convinced me to try a yoga class with her next week, says it will help me control my emotions and stay calm. I asked her if I could bring Mom, and she said yes.

And then there's Amy. She might be the nicest person I've ever met. The girl doesn't have a mean bone in her body. It took me a while to warm to her, but I will be a loyal friend to Amy when school starts. She is the one I misjudged the most. Maybe because I was jealous of how the boys looked at her, including Brett. It's funny, I never think about Brett anymore.

I watch Max eat his ice cream. Magic Max, with his wavy hair and blue braces like mine. He pushes me to try new things, cheers me on, comforts me when I'm sad or scared, always has time to talk. I once thought he was weird for being so into magic. Now I like it too, and I can't imagine not having him around.

But he won't be. He'll be in Pennsylvania soon. Our magic shows, our inside jokes, seeing him every day. No more.

Max spills some ice cream on his shirt, looks down, smiles. He's cute. I see it now. Maybe I always have. I wonder if Trina is right that he likes me.

Do I like him as more than a friend?

I've hugged him before, but tonight, hugging him made me feel like a mushy, melted puddle of goo, like an ice cream left out in the sun.

Maybe I do.

I, uh . . . I like you.
Like, *really* like you.

I should be happy. It's Drew's bar mitzvah party. I should be celebrating with everyone on the dance floor. But Max is on his way to Pennsylvania.

I keep checking my phone for texts from him, but it's Drew's Big Day. I put my phone down and force Max out of my mind.

Drew did a great job reading the Torah in synagogue earlier, which was as riveting as watching a snail cross the street. Now everyone is finished dancing the horah in their fancy dresses and suits, and sitting at the tables to catch their breath. The horah is a Jewish dance from ancient times done on festive occasions. What happens is everyone rushes the dance floor, joins hands, and dances around in crowded circles. Then they lift people in chairs and bounce them until someone gets hurt, usually because someone got a hernia from lifting the person in the chair.

Waiters serve the first course (some weird salad) while Dad gives his speech all about his wonderful, brilliant son, Drew. Drew walks up on stage and whispers in Dad's ear. Drew already gave his speech about his Torah portion. What is he doing?

Dad goes, "What's that? You want to say something? Sure."

Drew goes up to the microphone. "I just want to thank you, Mom and Dad, for teaching me what it means to be a person who stands up for what he believes. I don't believe in forcing anyone to do something against their will. So I just want to say in front of God and everybody here that I will not be participating in a flag football league, or any organized sports." He stares right at Dad when he says that. I've been joking about Drew becoming a man with this bar mitzvah stuff, but he sounds so sure of himself and confident, it almost seems like he has. "I know you mean well, Dad, wanting me to be good at sports, but I'm not." Mike, sitting next to me, snickers. I flick him in the back of the head. Hard. He tries to flick me back, but I scoot my chair out of his reach and keep my eyes fixed on Drew, who says, "What I am good at is movies. I think after you watch this, you'll all agree I have a pretty great family. Enjoy."

The lights dim. A screen behind Drew lights up. Then the movie starts.

It's fantastic. Plenty of the footage is of me, playing basketball on the driveway, playing football with Dad outside, making faces, writhing on the ground pretending to have a convulsion. Some of the clips are indoors, me horsing around in restaurants, rubbing Beth's belly, eating popcorn on the couch. Then there's Grandpa raising his glass, Mom taking a dinner roll out of Dad's hand, Grandma wiggling her skinny eyebrows, Grandpa's dentures coming loose. Those are the funny parts. But some of it is serious, like Beth holding up a pair of baby booties, me at the kitchen table trying to study, breaking a pencil on my head, Dad stocking shelves at the store, Mike kissing Beth and rubbing her belly, Grandma dabbing her eyes with a tissue, or Dad with his arm around Mom.

Watching, I feel something for my family I can only describe as love. Big, warm, mushy love. And maybe pride. I know I won't feel this way all the time, but right now, right this second, I know I'm pretty lucky to have my crazy family.

Then when I think the video is over, there's more. My friends and me in my room waving at the camera, then watching *The Breakfast Club* on Max's laptop, at Baskin-Robbins talking and laughing, Max and me performing in front of a group of clapping children, then holding hands and bowing slowly. I hug myself and soak up the images on-screen. That's what I should have posted on YouTube. Seeing Max up there gives me a dull ache in the pit of my stomach. I wish he was here.

What if he never comes back? What if we don't keep in touch?

My eyes get blurry with tears. I can't stop them. I wipe them off with a napkin.

The video ends. Drew steps down off the stage, so I get up from my seat at the *Titanic* table and run over to him. "That was awesome!" I tell him. "I loved it."

"The video or my speech?" he asks.

"Both," I answer. "And you."

"Thanks. Love you too." We're strangely silent for a few seconds. It's highly uncommon to say you love your sib, at least to their face. I rub the top of his head, giving him a noogie. He tries to give me one, but I duck. Good. Things are back to normal.

"Time to dance!" the MC shouts, and a fun song blasts through the speakers. Everyone moves to the dance floor. Kids flock near the stage, adults head to the bar. Trina, Amy, and I find each other and jump up and down. Mom and Dad let me invite them.

"I love your dress!" Trina shouts over the music.

"Thanks! Amy helped me with it!" Amy smiles as she dances around Trina and me. Who knew Amy could dance? She may not be good with words, but she has moves like Beyoncé! I tell her she should try out for the dance team. Trina's dancing, like mine, is eh. We whirl and twirl until everyone just starts jumping and fist pumping. I crash into some people by accident, but they don't seem to mind.

I have to give Mom props. Not only did she allow me to put a blue streak in my hair, she let me use Kool-Aid, which is *way* more permanent than chalk—it takes a couple of weeks to wash out. Plus, Mom did the dye job herself! Right in my bathroom sink! She said she wants us to spend more time doing stuff together. The way things are going, she might take me to a salon to use real dye someday. Fingers crossed.

Caitlin approaches me, Trina, and Amy on the dance floor, moving more awkwardly than Beth, who has one hand on her baby bump the whole time. Caitlin can't even keep the beat. But she's trying, and she's being nice to Trina and Amy. Caitlin is the one who told me which flavors of Kool-Aid to use (blue raspberry mixed with grape). We've been talking since she came home, and she hasn't insulted me yet. So far, so good. If anyone knows that people deserve a chance to try and change, it's me.

I leave the dance floor to go to the ladies' room. I

don't have to go, but Mom put a basket of toiletries and beauty products in the bathroom, and I might try the cologne because I'm sweaty from dancing/jumping.

In the lobby, the sight of him stops me in my tracks.

"MAX!"

He's sitting on his prop case, wearing a dress shirt and dress pants.

"I like your dress."

"Thanks."

My stomach flip-flops. It's not the kind of flip-flop you get from seeing a friend. It's the kind of flip-flop you get from seeing someone you have a crush on, a belly flop that goes on and on inside. I feel warm all of a sudden, even though the synagogue has excellent air-conditioning.

"What happened to Pennsylvania?" I ask.

He shakes his head. "It's . . . postponed. Indefinitely."

"But your mom—"

"She'll have to wait. It's complicated. I'll definitely get to see her, but she's not ready for me to live with her. I'm okay with it. I had a talk with my dad."

My eyes widen, surprised. "You had a talk with your dad?"

He runs his hand through his wavy hair. "Yeah. It's the first time he's listened to me in a long time."

Some of my parents' friends walk by, eyeing Max and me curiously. "So . . . for now, I'm not moving."

He's staying! He's staying!

"YAY!!" I shout. I can hear my heart beating double-time. I want to hug Max at this news, but somehow I'm frozen.

Finally, Max says, "Can we talk? In private?"

I lead him through the double doors to where the temple offices are and find a small room with the door open. Inside is a foldout bridge table, four chairs, and a vending machine. Max rests his prop case on the floor and sits on top of the table. I close the door and sit on the chair across from him. "Why do you have your prop case?" I ask.

"I remember you saying your mom was worried about having enough entertainment, so I thought maybe she'd like a magic show."

"Oh."

He clears his throat.

"So, what do you want to talk about?" I ask nervously.

He shifts his gaze to the door, then back to me. "I want to tell you that, uh . . ." His cheeks flush red like on the first day of Tony's class. "You're loud and hyper and you talk too much. You're always wiggling your feet or dropping or breaking something. The truth is, you're like a chimpanzee half the time."

I don't know what I was expecting, but it wasn't this. "Max, are you trying to start a fight? Because I could say a few things about you too, you know."

"No, I'm not trying to start a fight. I'm trying to say you make me laugh."

"I know that."

"You don't understand. No one has been able to do that since my mom left. My dad barely talks to me. My house is quieter than a cemetery. It's all I knew before I met you."

"Max, I—"

"Also, you're always interrupting." He stops, takes a breath. "But see, here's the thing. I like being around you. Because it doesn't matter where I am or what I'm doing . . ." He shrugs. "I'm just a little more happy when you're around. I, uh . . . I like you. Like, *really* like you." I don't have to ask if he means as more than a friend. That's exactly what he means. "When you asked me that first day of summer school if I thought you were cute? Even though you were just joking, the reason I got so embarrassed is because I *do* think you're cute. I always have."

!!!!!!!!!!!!!!

I want to stay calm and tell him I think he's cute too, and that I like him the same way, that he's the best thing that's happened to me this whole crazy summer. Instead, I jump up, sit on the table next to him, and throw my arms around him. I briefly wonder if I should try to kiss him or if he'll try to kiss me. I'm scared. I can tell Max feels the same way, judging by his red face. So we just hug. For a long time.

It feels nice.

And then the table makes this *ping* noise.

Followed by a louder *PING*.

And then collapses. With Max on top of it. And me on top of Max.

"Are you okay?" Max asks after we recover from the shock.

"Yeah. You?" We look down at our tangled arms and legs.

"I think so," he says.

About half a second passes before we both crack up. It's about another second before the door bursts open with Mom behind it. "What is going on in here?" She stops, suddenly registering me on Max on a broken table, and gasps. "Oh, hi, Max. Glad you could make it!"

"Hi, Mrs. Green," Max says from under me. "Um . . . we're working on a magic trick."

Mom raises an eyebrow.

"It's called the disappearing table," I add.

She crosses her arms. "Right." Max and I scramble up off the floor. Mom shoots us a stern look, but her eyes are twinkling. Then she spots Max's prop case. "Listen, you two, I'd be happy to pay you for a magic show. So, whenever you're ready . . ." Mom leaves.

I look at Max. "Ready?"

"Ready."

He takes my hand.

"Did you know ninety percent of the world's population kiss?" he asks.

I squeeze his hand. "Tell me about it later, Captain Trivia. We've got a show to do." We head toward the stage, and into the spotlight, together.

Author's Note

Someone recently asked me, "Why did you write *This Is Not the Abby Show*? Are you the *real* Abby?"

The answer to the first question is that I wrote this story because I wanted to show what it feels like to have ADHD, to help others have a better understanding of those who have it. I also wanted to show the power of friendship, and how much we grow when we spend time with people different from ourselves.

In answer to the second question, Abby is a mix of several people, including friends I had in school, students I've taught, my son Sam, and yes, a little of me. While I've never formally received a diagnosis of ADHD, a doctor did tell me that I meet a lot of the criteria.

One middle school friend of mine heavily inspired Abby's character. Kate (not her real name) was super smart, but she blurted out answers in class, was easily distracted, and broke everything, including our film projector. (Back in ye olde early 1980s, schools had projectors with old-timey film reels, because there was no such thing as DVDs or YouTube. I know. The horror. Are you okay? Breathe.) Looking back, I realize now that Kate probably had ADHD. She just wasn't diagnosed or treated for it, which was often the case back then.

Kate was hilarious, but sometimes her jokes crossed the border into mean territory. If I tripped, she'd scream, "SMOOTH MOVE, EX-LAX!" Like Abby, Kate wasn't deliberately hurtful or a bully. When I told Kate that she'd hurt my feelings, she felt terrible to the point of tears and always apologized sincerely. Having "no filter"—that is, having difficulty editing verbal comments, or having "conversational accidents"—is typical of many with ADHD. I think a huge obstacle facing people like Kate and Abby is that they are often misunderstood by classmates, teachers, and family members. That can lead to a lot of sadness and to feelings of hopelessness.

But people like Kate and Abby are often gifted with the ability to sense things others don't. One afternoon, while I was sitting in Mrs. Queen's math class, I spotted Kate out the window, leaving Mr. P's portable classroom and sprinting toward us like a rocket. What shocked me the most was that she was running on the grass, which was strictly off-limits at our school. No one broke the Stay-off-the-Grass rule. Ever.

Kate trampled over the forbidden grass as if she were running for her life. She was, in fact, running to save a life, but not her own. She burst into our room, shouting, "HELP! MR. P'S HAVING A HEART ATTACK!"

I found out later that by the time Mr. P fell to the floor and his students realized what was happening, Kate had already left the building, ten steps ahead of everyone. Kate's fast thinking and her perceptive, impulse-driven, rule-breaking actions saved Mr. P's life that day. Those are all ADHD traits. As Abby points out in chapter one: *I do pay attention, just not to the same things as everyone else.*

It was important to me to include plenty of humor in Abby's story. I don't think it's a coincidence that so many stars of comedy have ADHD, including Howie Mandel, Channing Tatum, and Jim Carrey. Do they use humor to cover up their ADHD symptoms or to cope with the sadness that comes with it when things aren't going well? Possibly. Is their quick wit a result of a fast-thinking, extraordinary brain? Definitely.

The self-confidence that Abby gains in her story was inspired by my son Sam. There will always be those who don't understand ADHD, like Mr. Finsecker and Abby's Aunt Roz. It would be nice if everyone were understanding and supportive like Tony, but when someone isn't, it's important to try not to let it get to you. Sam told me once: "If someone has the wrong idea about ADHD, that says more about them than it does about me." How true. Sam's older brother, Louis, once wrote in a letter to Sam: *Some of the things you do may not always make sense to me. However, that is what makes you a unique individual.* Louis showed me that adults can learn a lot from kids when it comes to embracing differences in others.

Do You Have ADHD?

Some of you may have just read *This Is Not the Abby Show* and are thinking, "Hold on. Abby isn't anything like me, and I have ADHD. What's up with that?" That could very well be true. The tricky thing about this medical condition is that it presents differently in each person. Not everyone is as hyperactive as Abby. Some people have the more inattentive type of ADHD. Some have extreme cases, while some have mild cases. That's why treatment varies, and there are different kinds of doctors you can go to for help.

To a person with ADHD, a fly in the classroom may be as important as the teacher talking. Judging what's important and what should be ignored is extremely difficult. Imagine the inside of your brain as the TV wall at an electronics store, with each TV broadcasting a different program. Which TVs do you turn off? Which do you leave on? That's ADHD.

Maybe you're the kid able to sit quietly in class, but there is so much going on in your head, it drowns out everything around you. Or maybe you are twice exceptional, like Abby, gifted in a particular academic area in addition to having ADHD. That's very common. Some of the greatest thinkers, innovators, artists, and leaders in world history are believed to have had ADHD, including Albert Einstein, Ben Franklin, Eleanor Roosevelt, and John Lennon. Here are a few alive today you may recognize: Justin Timberlake, musician and actor; Michael Phelps, most-winning Olympic gold medalist of all time; David Neeleman, founder of JetBlue Airways; and Adam Levine, musician and actor.

Many exceptionally intelligent, creative people credit ADHD with the key to their success. They may wear mismatched socks, have no clue where they left their cell phone, and leave the door unlocked, but they have unique and wonderful qualities, and so do you.

Here is a list of qualities that many people with ADHD possess. Which of these apply to you?

    creative
    spontaneous

honest
energetic
fun
compassionate
imaginative
brave
curious
able to think outside the box
daring
helpful, eager to volunteer
warm, friendly
interested in a variety of topics

For more information about ADHD, check out these resources:

Help4ADHD.org
ADDwarehouse.com
CHADD.org
Additudemag.com

Visit me at debbiereedfischer.com. I'd love to hear from you!

Acknowledgments

This book couldn't have been written without the help and support of many people. Thanks go to:

My talented editor, Rebecca Weston. You understood Abby from the first draft, and I'm so grateful my manuscript landed on your desk. Your insights made me dig deeper to get to the heart of the story and made this process enjoyable. Kate Gartner and illustrator Tuesday Mourning, for capturing Abby and her friends so perfectly for this cover, and Trish Parcell, for the beautiful interior design. Everyone at Random House Children's Books/Delacorte Press.

My agent extraordinaire, Steven Chudney, for believing in me and guiding the way. Whether answering my emails with lightning speed or handling contracts, you are the best.

Alex Flinn, for your advice, and for sharing so much of your personal journey with me while I wrote this book. Dorian Cirrone, for your keen observations throughout many drafts. Thank you both for always being there for me. I treasure our emails, texts, and conversations. (Don't worry, I deleted everything.)

Big hugs to Joyce Sweeney, my mentor and long-time friend, and to Laurie Taddanio, Flora Doone, Gloria Rothstein, and Lane Fredrickson. *Muchas gracias* to Linda Rodriguez-Bernfeld and Gaby Triana for leading our Florida SCBWI chapter with such dedication. All my SCBWI friends, online and locally, I'd be lost without your camaraderie. Your talent motivates me to up my game.

Dr. Judith Aronson-Ramos, for your expertise, insight, and for clarifying questions regarding ADHD. Dr. Stacy Davids, for coming through at the eleventh hour with helpful details. Dr. Rona Bernstein, for your personal encouragement when this book was just an idea.

Sydney Altschul, for her unique personal perspective.

Loren Stein, for being my good-luck charm after a random meeting at Office Depot. Our conversation about stand-up comedy, creativity, and ADHD made a big impact on this book. Sherry Grossman, for reminding me why humor is important for kids in Abby's situation, and for important medical details.

All the Abbies I've known, for opening my eyes to both the challenges and joys of being twice exceptional. You can't be a shadow if you're born to be a light. Shine, shine, shine.

My biggest fans, Sara and Donald Reed, also known as my parents, for always allowing me to read whatever I wanted and for encouraging me to write. I am forever grateful. All my family and friends who cheer me on.

I owe a debt of gratitude to my husband, Eric. It's not easy to be married to an author. Thank you for not minding when my alarm clock goes off at four in the morning because I need to get up and write, for taking me seriously when I discuss characters as if they're real, and for making me laugh when I want to cry. Okay, I'll stop thanking you now. Actually, no, I won't. I can never thank you enough. I love you.

Finally, saving the best for last, a giant hug to my biggest blessings, my sons. Louis, for giving me wise counsel on anything teen-related, such as the 411 on which sayings aren't cool anymore (like "the 411," for example). Also, for helping me by ordering pizzas or taking your brother out when I'm on deadline. Sam, thanks for naming Abby, and for giving me the inside scoop about life in middle school. You guys both fill my life with purpose, pride, and a lot of information about sports. I love you to the moon and back. I'm very lucky to be your mother.

About the Author

DEBBIE REED FISCHER is the author of novels for teens and tweens, and has been praised by *Kirkus Reviews* for balancing "weighty issues with a sharp wit." When she isn't writing, Debbie is chatting on-line with her readers, teaching writing workshops, playing guitar, singing with her band, running, or watching just about anything on TV. She has lived in England, Greece, and Israel, and now lives in South Florida with her husband and two sons, who don't mind eating takeout when she is on deadline. Visit her at debbiereedfischer.com.